STONES
IN
WATER

STONES IN WATER

DONNA JO NAPOLI

SCHOLASTIC INC.

New York   Toronto   London   Auckland   Sydney
Mexico City   New Delhi   Hong Kong

ISBN 0-439-14122-2

Text copyright © 1997 by Donna Jo Napoli.
Cover illustration copyright © 1997 by Scott Hunt.
All rights reserved.
Published by Scholastic Inc., 555 Broadway, New York, NY 10012,
by arrangement with Dutton Children's Books, a division of Penguin Putnam Inc.
SCHOLASTIC and associated logos are trademarks and/or registered trademarks of
Scholastic Inc.

12 11 10 9 8 7 6 5 4 3 2 1   9/9 0 1 2 3 4/0

Printed in the U.S.A.   40

First Scholastic printing, September 1999

Designed by Semadar Megged

For Guido and Suzy

ACKNOWLEDGMENTS

I thank Oleksa-Myron Bilaniuk, Etta Gold, Pieter Judson, Lucia Monfried, Rosaria Munson, Larissa Zaleska-Onyshkevych, Lubomyr Onyshkevych, Daphne Riley, Richard Tchen, Louise Tilly, Tom Whitman, and Ed Gaynor's class at the Swarthmore-Rutledge School in 1995–96 for doing their best to save me from errors of history and heart. I thank the International Committee of the Red Cross for allowing me access to their archives in Geneva in the summer of 1995. I thank all the patient librarians who managed to dig up books for me on the most obscure topics—from those at Swarthmore College to those at the many libraries in Geneva and in Venice. And I thank my family—Barry, Elena, Mike, Nick, Eva, and Robert Furrow—for all the terrible usuals.

This story is based loosely (very, very loosely) on experiences of Guido Fullin during World War II, and I thank both him and his wife, Susan Curcio, for talking with me about them and about this story. I also thank Franco Berlanda for talking with me about an early draft of this story and about his experiences as a *partigiano,* and for giving me materials to read by Ugo Pecchioli.

Contents

STONES
IN
WATER

THE FILM

"It's the money, isn't it?"

Of course it was the money. Roberto put both hands in his pockets and looked down. "No."

Memo closed the fingertips of his right hand together and shook them under Roberto's nose. "Don't give me that bull. Okay, listen, I'll lend you the money, and you'll do me a little favor, right?"

Roberto looked up. A favor? "Tell me about the film first."

"It's good. American. Lots of cowboys." Memo smiled slyly. "You want to go, right?"

Roberto had been to only two American films in his life. Yes, he wanted to go. But favors for Memo had gotten him in trouble before. "What favor?"

"Tell me, you want to go or not?"

"I want to go."

Memo grinned. "Okay, now we understand each other." He threw an arm around Roberto's shoulder. "Your cousin Teresa. All I want is for you to tell her I'm a nice guy, right? She should think about maybe going for a walk with me. Maybe a boat ride out to the Lido. Just tell her."

Robert stared at Memo. His cousin Teresa was already in love with Paolo. Memo should have known that; he knew just about everything that went on anywhere in Venice. But all Roberto had to do to earn the money for the movie ticket was say yes. Only it would be a lie. "Teresa loves Paolo."

Memo's arm dropped off Roberto's shoulder. "You're kidding." His face went slack for a minute. Then he shook his head. "I guess you'll have to steal the money from your old man."

Cowboys. Gunfights in the streets of the Old West. Women in tight-fitting bodices. Who knew when Roberto would get a chance like this again? Especially with the war going on. When Italy declared war on America last December—just days after the Japanese bombed the American Pearl Harbor—everyone said that would be the end of American things in Italy for a while. It was a miracle an American film was being shown anywhere anymore. Roberto plucked at Memo's sleeve. "Lend me the money, and I'll find a way to pay you back later."

Memo lifted his chin. "When I get my next girl, you'll give us a moonlight gondola ride. Good deal, right?"

Memo thought all his ideas were "right," but they weren't. This idea, for example, was a problem. Roberto's father was a *gondoliere*, just as his father had been before him and as his father had been before him, going back as far as anyone knew. Roberto would never be a *gondoliere* because his big brother Sergio would be the one to inherit the license when his father was ready to give it up. But Roberto knew how to handle a gondola. He could easily give Memo a ride. So long as his father didn't find out. His father didn't like him using the gondola like that. If Roberto damaged it, his father would be out of work till it was fixed. Still, the chances of damaging it were small, particularly at night, when the canals were close to empty. Roberto shook Memo's hand. "Sure."

"I'll meet you at the Scalzi bridge in a half hour. We can walk the highway."

Roberto ran through the back alleys and cut across the Jewish ghetto. The ghetto was a calm and beautiful place, and Roberto made a point of passing through whenever he could. In spring the smell of hot matzoh in the bakery made his mouth water.

"Hey, Roberto, what's your hurry?"

Roberto stopped.

Samuele leaned against the water cistern in the center

of the open area—the *campo*. He smiled at Roberto. Samuele was in the same grade as Memo and Roberto, and they'd all known each other forever. It was already the start of June, and they would graduate from middle school in a few weeks. Probably none of them was going on to high school—the *liceo*—next year. They were too young to be soldiers, and the handful of civilian jobs around were quickly grabbed up by men, so the three boys were in the same boat: They'd spend the next few years scrounging up opportunities for work, trying to stay out of trouble. They understood each other well. "Come on, tell me," said Samuele. "What're you doing?"

Roberto walked over to him. "There's an American film, a western, in Mestre."

"Yeah?" Samuele's eyes lit up.

"If you've got the money, come with us. Memo and me. We're meeting at the Scalzi bridge as soon as I get my shoes on."

"I'll be at the bridge." Samuele ran across the *campo* and into his house.

Roberto crossed the bridge out of the ghetto, ran through alleys, and crossed two more bridges. He opened the door and took the two flights up, two steps at a time.

Mamma was in the kitchen with the radio blaring news—something about a new British bomb that weighed more than a thousand kilograms. She used to listen to music and dance around the house. But ever since Italy had signed the Tripartite Pact with Germany and Japan, Mamma listened only to war news.

Roberto walked softly through the hall and slipped into his bedroom.

His big brother Sergio was stretched out on the bed. Roberto stopped, surprised. For months now, Sergio had spent his Saturdays drilling in Campo San Stefano. Roberto had gone a few times himself. They learned how to march; how to carry rifles; how to make the kicks of martial arts, complete with shouts and grunts. And, best of all, they learned how to box. Sergio should have been at the drills now.

Roberto snatched his shoes and went for the door.

In a flash Sergio jumped up and grabbed Roberto by the arm. "Just where do you think you're going?"

"Mestre."

"What's in Mestre?"

"A film."

"I know about films. Films don't start till the afternoon."

"We're walking. It'll take us that long just to get there."

"Who's 'we'?"

"Memo and me. Maybe others." Roberto didn't mention Samuele by name. Roberto's parents had told him to be careful about the Jews. At first he wasn't allowed to go into their homes. Then he wasn't allowed to be seen in public with Samuele. But he did it all the same. He liked Samuele.

And, anyway, Mamma was still friends with Samuele's mother—he knew that, no matter what she said. In March the two of them had joined other women from the neighborhoods of Cannaregio and Castello and walked through the streets of Venice protesting the war. Mamma said it had nothing to do with politics—it was a matter of work and food. Italy was suffering from this war.

Sergio's eyes narrowed. "How're you paying for it?"

"Memo's paying."

"That little thief—stealing jobs that should go to men. Someone's family will go hungry tonight because of him."

Roberto squirmed at the accusation. Memo did the usual errands that boys did—he carried groceries for old women and walked dogs for shut-ins. But he also did other errands for a handful of coins—delivering telegrams to people who lived too far for the old telegraph man to walk to, even delivering money for services rendered. They were the kinds of errands that used to go to men. But men demanded decent pay. So Memo won the jobs. But surely no one went hungry because of him.

Sergio raised an eyebrow. "Why's Memo paying for you, anyway?"

"I'm doing him a favor."

"Is the movie a Western?"

"Yeah."

Sergio let go of Roberto's arm.

Roberto snuck back along the hall. Then he ran downstairs. He sat on the bottom step and tied his shoes. He ran out the door.

Sergio caught up with him, his shoelaces flapping.

"What're you doing?" said Roberto.

"What's it look like? I'm coming along."

"You're coming? But why aren't you with the other guys, drilling in the *campo?*"

"Both my black shirts are dirty."

Everyone wore black shirts to the drills—to show they were fascists. Even their teachers wore black shirts. Roberto's mother scrubbed the clothes every day, but lately Sergio had gotten in the habit of throwing his dirty clothes on the floor—and Mamma had staged a strike, refusing to wash anything that wasn't in the dirty-clothes basket.

Roberto twisted his mouth in worry. He didn't want Sergio coming along, bossing him around. "Where'd you get the money?"

"Memo will pay for me, too."

"How come?"

"You'll do him the favor twice."

"That's not fair."

"That's what big brothers are for: to teach you the facts of life. Fact number one: Life isn't fair."

They ducked down an alley without even a glance of agreement passing between them. It was a given that they should avoid Signora Rossini's eye at the newsstand. She was friends with their mother and the biggest busybody in town. If Mamma knew they were off spending money, even someone else's money, when they should have been hustling up odd jobs or drilling in the *campo*, she'd yell at them for a half hour straight. Or she'd cry. Roberto hated the crying more than the yelling.

Mamma cried a lot since the war began. Tourists were the ones who paid big money for rides in gondolas. And for the past two years tourists had hardly come at all. The only rides his father gave these days were short jogs across the canals for men in a rush on their way to work.

Samuele and Memo were already on the bridge.

"Let's get going," said Samuele.

"Hold on." Sergio took Memo by the arm with one hand and Roberto by the arm with the other. "Who invited the Jew?"

Roberto pulled his arm away. "He's my friend."

"He's a Jew, you idiot. You know about Hitler and Jews. Even someone with his head in the clouds like you has to know that." Sergio slapped his forehead with his palm. "Fact number two: Don't play with fire."

"I've got my own money," said Samuele. "I'll walk there by myself." He leaned his back against the wall of the bridge, his elbows jutting out over the water, his lanky legs crossed at the ankle. A vein in his neck stood out and throbbed.

Roberto moved beside Samuele. "I'll walk with you."

Memo jerked his shoulders uncomfortably and adjusted his collar. "Yeah, I'll walk with the two of you."

"Just hold it, everyone." Sergio extended both hands, fingers spread. "If the police stop you, what will you say?"

"Nothing," said Memo. "There's nothing to say. No one's going to bother with three schoolboys, right?"

"Wrong." Sergio shook his head. "You're all pathetic. Roberto and Memo, you walk ahead. I'll walk with Samuele. If anyone stops us, we're two separate groups, and I speak for me and Samuele. Got it?"

Roberto looked at Samuele. It wasn't a bad idea. Samuele was almost as tall as Sergio, and if he kept his head down, no one would realize he was younger.

Samuele shrugged. "Sure."

"Just one more thing," said Sergio. "Memo's paying for me, too . . ."

Memo opened his mouth to protest.

". . . 'cause Roberto's going to do that little favor twice, aren't you, Berti-boy?"

"Yeah, sure," said Roberto. What else could he say? Anyway, the idea of meeting the police had set him on edge. It would be better to have Sergio along.

Memo nodded.

Sergio held out his hand. "Give me that." He thrust his chin toward Samuele's armband.

Roberto wanted to object. All Jews were required to wear the Star of David armband. And even though no one seemed to care much about it in Venice, if Samuele was caught without it in Mestre, something might happen. A fine maybe. Something.

But Samuele didn't speak up—so Roberto held his tongue. Samuele pulled the band down his arm and handed it to Sergio.

Sergio crossed to the end of the bridge and looked up and down the path by the restaurant there. It was too early for lunch, and restaurants these days didn't get much business anyway: There was no one about. Sergio went to an outdoor table and tucked the band under the center support of the table. "We'll be back before they close up and put the tables inside."

Samuele nodded.

They made their way to the Serenissima highway. The sun beat down. The water of the laguna was low and clear. Schools of black minnows darted about. The water was so shallow that Roberto saw a group of crabs scuttling around the carcass of a snapper. A lone rowboat rocked gently. The occupant was out of sight.

The train rumbled by on the tracks to their left. Roberto

jumped at the sound. He kept his eyes on the highway. Who would be the first to spot the police?

But nothing passed except an occasional truck and dozens of bicycles piled high with boxes.

The theatre was near the train station, and when they finally arrived, there was no line outside. That meant they were late. They bought their tickets and hurried in, hushing as they entered the dark. The newsreel boomed. They followed the little light of the usher down the aisle and scooted past the feet of strangers to the middle of a row.

Roberto wound up behind a tall kid. He leaned toward Samuele so he could see.

"Want to switch with me?" whispered Samuele. He got up and they changed seats.

"Thanks." Roberto could see everything now. He loved the big theatre screen. He felt surrounded by it, as though he were there, in the middle of the fast-moving picture.

War news flashed across the screen. German soldiers marched in the Crimea. They captured Kertch. Everyone was afraid of the Germans. Meanwhile, an American airplane dropped bombs over the German town Cologne. None of the bombs struck anything important, though. The American and British air forces were incompetent, despite their larger bombers. And now the Japanese were dropping bombs someplace far away in the East.

Roberto knew the geography of Europe and western

Asia—he could place the Crimean battle on the Black Sea and the German battle along the Rhine River. But his teachers hadn't talked much about the geography of Asia. Still, he sat up straight when he heard about the Japanese bombs—they weighed five hundred kilograms. Roberto furrowed his brows—that was half the weight of the British bomb he'd heard about on the radio. How could the Axis forces win if the enemy had bigger bombs? But the newsreel said that everyone was surrendering to the Germans or the Japanese. So it was okay. Italy would come out okay.

Italian troops flapped their caps at the camera, smiling wide. They were stationed in Tunis, in North Africa, and, despite the fact that they had been driven back from Abyssinia last fall, they were doing their part valiantly. It wouldn't be long before that whole area fell to the Axis powers.

Roberto's eyes slowly adjusted to the dark. He looked around. The theatre was packed with boys. No girls, as far as he could tell. Westerns weren't so popular with girls—plus most girls' mothers wouldn't let them go to the movies without chaperones. Several rows ahead he saw a few boys from Venice. But most of the kids were from Mestre and the little villages outside. He didn't see an adult in the group.

The newsreel ended and the Western began. Roberto stared up at the title and actors' names on the huge screen.

Suddenly the lights went on. Roberto blinked against the brightness. Boys groaned and hooted in complaint. He joined in.

The hoots mixed with screams. German soldiers marched down the aisles. Soldiers, here in the theatre. Roberto focused on their stomping boots. The boots seemed absurd in the early summer heat. Everything was loud, deafening—the confusion made Roberto feel stupid and somehow distant, detached. He forced himself to look around and pay attention. Rifles swung from straps over the soldiers' shoulders. They shouted orders. Half the audience was standing by now, pushing, trying to get out.

Roberto's heart pounded. He reached across Samuele and grabbed Sergio's hand. "What's going on?"

Sergio stood up and leaned over the three boys. "Keep your mouths shut and do what everyone else does."

Samuele let Roberto squish past him so that he was right behind Sergio. But Sergio pulled his hand away and moved toward the closest aisle. He spoke out of the side of his mouth without looking at Roberto. "Stay close. Just stay close."

THE TRAIN

Everyone pressed into the aisles, Roberto on Sergio's heels, Memo and Samuele close behind.

The soldiers shouted at the stumbling crowd. They hit the boys' legs with wooden batons. Someone finally understood and yelled in Venetian dialect for everyone to go single file.

Another boy jammed between Sergio and Roberto in the line. Roberto looked around in panic. At least Samuele was right behind Roberto, and Memo right behind him. When they got out of the theatre, Roberto would catch up with Sergio.

But when they got out of the theatre, more soldiers were waiting for them. They shouted and pushed and split the boys into two groups, clearly by age. Sergio went with the older boys. Roberto called to him, but his voice was lost in the din.

"Keep your mouth shut," hissed Memo. "Do what Sergio said."

"Why?" said Roberto. "The Germans are on our side."

"The Germans are on their own side," said Samuele.

A boy near Roberto shouted, "I have to get home now."

"Me, too," shouted another.

And everyone was shouting, "I have to get home now."

Bang!

The crowd hushed. Roberto looked around, frantic. But no one had fallen. A soldier must have fired into the air.

The soldiers shouted and marched them down the street. Every Easter Roberto went with his family to visit cousins who lived in the hills southwest of Padova. His cousin Guido herded a flock by himself. Roberto envied Guido and often imagined being him. But now he had the sensation of being one of the sheep, freshly shorn and wild-eyed, pressed on from all sides. His heart thumped.

They went into the Mestre train station. Thank heavens, they were about to be sent home. Now he understood: This was their punishment for going to see an American film in the middle of the war. In a minute, the soldiers would separate out the ones who were going east to Venice from the ones who were going west to the villages outside Mestre. Roberto didn't even have the change for the train ticket. And he didn't want to borrow more money from Memo. But if he was lucky, no one would check to see if he had a ticket. And if he got caught, he'd explain what happened. It would all be okay.

Roberto breathed more slowly. He looked around for the other groups of Venetian boys. They might as well all get together now. "Come on," he said to Memo and Samuele. He turned around and pressed toward the rear of the crowd.

A soldier shouted at him—an Italian soldier. Things couldn't go too badly now that Italian soldiers were here, too. Roberto moved toward the soldier in relief, but the soldier yelled and told Roberto to go with the crowd.

Memo jerked hard on the back of Roberto's pants.

Roberto turned forward and let himself be pushed by the crowd down the steps and up again, onto the platform by the second track, to a waiting train. The boys in his group were loaded into one train car. The older boys were loaded into a separate one. It made no sense—they didn't all live in the same direction.

No one took seats. They stood at the windows in clumps and looked out at the soldiers on the train platforms. Two German soldiers got on their train car. The engines revved up. The doors shut. The train started. It headed west.

Roberto shook his head. "We're going the wrong way." His stomach lurched.

"I should have run for it." Samuele stared at Roberto with terror in his eyes. "I should have run while I had a chance."

Roberto shook his head again. He clenched his teeth against the fear. "This is a mistake. It's just a big mistake."

The car full of boys was noisy and hot.

"My mother's going to worry," someone said loudly. "I'll never get home on time."

Voices of agreement chimed in. No one wanted to risk his mother's wrath or tears. People swapped mother stories.

Roberto could imagine his own mother carrying on crazy-like, what with both him and Sergio showing up late. She imagined danger everywhere.

"Look at them," said Samuele, with a small nod toward the soldiers at the end of the car. "They can't be more than twenty years old—you can tell in spite of their fancy uniforms." He blinked and whispered hoarsely, "Two of them to a whole carload of us."

The two German soldiers sat on the last row of seats. They smoked. One of them yawned, showing clean white teeth.

"They have guns." Memo sank onto a seat.

Samuele sat down beside him.

Roberto stayed standing, watching the cows go by. He stopped listening to the boys around him. These German soldiers were making trouble for him. His father would be enraged. The only saving grace was that Sergio had done it, too. Sergio, as the older brother, would bear the brunt of the punishment.

Pretty soon Roberto could see buildings ahead. He sat. "We're already at Padova."

Samuele got up and moved down the aisle away from the soldiers.

One of the soldiers called to him.

Samuele didn't look back. Roberto knew he was heading for the door.

The soldier stood up.

Roberto quickly followed Samuele. He heard Memo right behind him. His mouth went dry and his chest tightened. But if Samuele was going to get off the train, so was he. He'd done nothing wrong—nothing more than go to an American film. And look what trouble he was in now. Memo always had money on him, sure, but he'd never have enough to buy three train tickets back to Venice. They'd have to walk most of the night to get home. Unless they were lucky enough to hitch a ride.

The soldier called to them in German.

The train was slowing down.

The soldier shouted now. He ran down the aisle, pushed past Roberto and Memo, and grabbed Samuele's arm. He spun him around, jabbering German. He slammed him against the side of a seat.

"Hey!" said Memo. He yanked on the soldier's sleeve.

He unbuttoned his shorts. "We have to use the bathroom. That's allowed, right?"

The soldier looked at Memo.

Memo exposed himself and pointed at the toilet cabin at the end of the car. "Pee!"

"Ah." The soldier gave a quick nod. He let go of Samuele.

The boys squeezed into the toilet cabin. Roberto swung the door shut, but the soldier put his boot on the doorsill and kept it from latching. Roberto leaned against the door from the inside. What was going on? When would the soldiers let them off? He pressed the back of his head against the door and pushed with all his strength.

Memo used the toilet. "You, too. Hurry," he said to Samuele. "Use it now, when there's only us to see."

Samuele used the toilet.

Roberto stared at Samuele's circumsized penis. Of course, he'd seen it before. But he hadn't thought about how it marked him as a Jew, no matter what he said, no matter where he was. If anyone found out, Samuele would be in serious trouble. He should have never agreed to let Sergio take the Star of David band off his arm. Samuele had broken the law.

It was Roberto's turn now. "Look." He took himself with both hands. "Hold your hands this way to cover yourself."

Samuele nodded.

"That was dumb." Memo cleared his throat and looked steadily at Samuele. "If you do something like that again, I won't follow you."

"Sergio said to do what everyone else does." Roberto moved closer to Samuele. "Sergio knows about these things."

Samuele set his jaw. But he nodded again.

They opened the door.

The soldier stepped aside and the boys went back to their seats.

The train stopped.

"Let us off," whined a boy near the door.

The other German soldier barked something at him.

The doors opened and more boys filed in. They called out in bewilderment and anger. They used Padovano dialect, which was a lot like Venetian.

Two more German soldiers got on. The doors shut.

They made three more stops that afternoon and evening: at Verona, Trento, and Bolzano. Each time, the train took on more Italian boys and more German soldiers. The boys exclaimed in dialects that were increasingly different from Roberto's language—but he understood anyway: They said the same things the boys from Mestre and Venice said when they'd first boarded the train.

The new boys jammed in, six to a bench seat that was intended to hold two adults. Several stood at the windows,

Roberto among them. Once, when they rounded a curve going through the Dolomite mountains, Roberto counted the train cars. Seven. Seven cars full of Italian boys heading up into the peaks. At the next curve he tried to see into the car behind his. The faces at the windows stood out distinct in the evening glow—but none of them was Sergio's. Roberto waved anyway, just in case Sergio was watching for him.

The mountains cut up through the air, proud and clean. These mountains that Roberto had heard so much about and had promised himself he'd see someday. Now he was seeing them. He blinked the tears from his eyes. There was no telling how he'd get home from here and how long it would take. There was no telling what punishment his father would give. He'd never done anything so terrible in his life.

Hunger made him irritable. Some of the boys who had gotten on the train at a later stop hadn't missed a meal. But Roberto hadn't eaten since breakfast. He had skipped the midday meal so that he could walk to the theatre in Mestre. His stomach growled. Loudly. He looked at Memo.

Memo looked back at him with big eyes.

Roberto's stomach growled again.

A smile crept across Memo's face.

Roberto's stomach growled again.

Memo laughed.

Roberto's irritation disappeared. He laughed, too. Everything was awful—but he laughed anyway.

Memo stood up and leaned beside Roberto, their faces to the open window. They watched the evergreens whip past.

"We're going to be soldiers," said a boy a few seats down. He spoke in the dialect of Mestre. "That's it, I bet. My uncle's a soldier."

"We can't be soldiers. You have to be eighteen."

"Uh-uh. Lots of younger boys have joined up. My brother did, and he was only seventeen then."

"So did my brother," said the boy beside him. "But he's twenty. He has so many medals, he doesn't know where to pin them all."

"The boy who lives upstairs from me goes to the infantry academy. He does gymnastics and he goes on bike rides in the Apennine Mountains. And when they blow trumpets, he has to wake up, or eat, or"—he giggled—"go to the bathroom."

The boys laughed.

"He loves it. He's stronger than he ever was."

"*Viva Il Duce!*" shouted a boy in school Italian.

"*Viva la guerra!*" shouted another boy.

"Greece is behind us," said the boy whose brother was twenty.

"What do you mean?" asked another.

"Don't you know how it's been? The Germans have been winning all the battles, while we Italians got whipped by the Greeks. My brother told me. But the shame is over." He lifted his chin with pride. "We're going to Germany. We'll fight beside the Germans and we'll win, too. Italians will win, too."

Someone sang "L'Inno a Roma." Most of the boys in the train car joined in. It was a song everyone knew from school. And now they sang "Fischia il Sasso" and "Giovinezza," songs to show what loyal citizens they were, what good fascists. Roberto sang along. But he didn't want to be a soldier, whether the Italians were losing or winning. And, anyway, he had to tell his parents if he was going off to war. He couldn't just leave like that.

They arrived at the border.

"We can't go across the Austrian border," Roberto whispered in Memo's ear.

"It's not Austria anymore. It's all part of Germany now."

"It doesn't matter. We can't cross any border. We have no documents on us. It's against the law."

The train stopped.

The entire train car fell silent.

The Austrian officials just looked at them.

"I'm getting off." A boy who had been sitting without talking most of the way stood up. He spoke loudly. "I'm not going any farther. I'm going home."

"Me, too."

"Me, too."

The three boys who had spoken walked down the aisle.

A soldier shouted. He stomped up behind the boys. But instead of grabbing them, he pushed them ahead of him.

Roberto tensed up. "They're getting off the train. Oh, they're really getting off. Let's do it, too. Fast."

Samuele stood behind Roberto and Memo. He quickly hooked his arms through theirs and looked over their shoulders out the window. "Wait."

"What do you mean, wait?" said Roberto. "You're the one who tried to get off at Padova."

"And it was stupid then," said Memo.

Samuele nodded. "Let's see what happens here first."

"What could happen?" said Roberto. "We can't cross the border without a passport. Everyone knows that. They can't make us go." He tried to pull away, but Samuele held him fast.

The soldier pushed the three boys along the train platform until they were outside the center of their train car. Another soldier came up and shoved at them from the other direction. The boys stood on the platform between the two soldiers. The three of them looked from one to the other. They said things Roberto couldn't catch. They jerked their heads from one soldier to the other, half crazed by now.

Roberto knew they were in deep trouble—terrifying trouble. "It's unfair," he said under his breath. "The boys are right. We can't cross the border. It's against the law."

The soldier who had pushed them off the train car turned to the boys who were still in the train, almost all of whom were now pressed in layers, staring out the windows. He shouted in German—fast and harsh. Then he held out his pistol and shot one of the boys in the head. Red spray fanned out in front of the boy as he fell forward. People screamed. One of the other two boys broke away and ran. The soldier shot him in the back. Then he shot the third boy in the head. They fell dead on the platform. Pools of blood widened around their bodies.

The soldier held his pistol in the air and shook it as he shouted again at the boys in the train cars. His voice was the only noise heard.

Roberto clutched the Saint Christopher medal on the chain around his neck. Christopher was the patron saint of travelers. Roberto squeezed so hard, the medal cut his fingers. He looked down. The salt of his tears stung as it mixed with his blood. "It's against the law," whispered Roberto, knowing his words were stupid, saying them anyway. "It's against the law."

Memo looked at Roberto. "There are no more laws."

PICKS

The sudden braking jerked Roberto awake. Memo's head rested on his right shoulder. Samuele's head was in his lap. The rocking of the train had been like the rocking of a gondola—almost soothing. But now it was over. Roberto rubbed his eyes.

Memo woke an instant later. He looked around as if he didn't know where he was.

Roberto shook Samuele awake.

The three of them stood at the window with the other three boys from their bench seat. The sign on the station read MÜNCHEN.

"Munich," said one of the other boys. The boy said a few more things in a dialect Roberto didn't recognize, but the gist of it was easy enough to understand—they had arrived at the Bavarian capital of Germany.

"Good," whispered Samuele to Roberto. "I've got to pee, and I've always wanted to pee on German soil."

Roberto could use a bathroom himself. The stench of urine made the air heavy. He looked down at Samuele's pants, but they were dry. Now he smelled feces, too. And everywhere the sour smell of dried sweat assailed him. His stomach turned. He was suddenly glad it was empty.

The doors opened. The soldiers yapped orders at the boys, but without energy; they sounded like tired dogs. One of them put both hands behind his neck, elbows forward, and stretched. He yawned. Maybe the soldiers hadn't slept at all.

The soldiers stood up and yapped louder. Now they swung their batons, whapping a shoulder, cracking across a back. The boys filed off the train and onto the platforms. Roberto thought of the boys who'd been shot at the border. His stomach turned again. He said nothing. He would do nothing to call attention to himself—that's what Sergio had meant, he now realized. Everyone seemed to be following the same strategy. They huddled together, silent in the cool wet of predawn, their knees sticking out of their short pants like naked pine trunks on the Lido in Venice.

A soldier walked up and down in front of them. He wore the same high black boots, the same wide black belt, the same armband with a swastika, as the other soldiers. But he had a black patch on each collar tip with two white zigzag lines. And his helmet had the same two zigzag lines in black on a white background. The soldier spoke loudly. He held his crotch. Then he put one hand to his open mouth, as though he was putting something in it. He chewed big.

The boys nodded. Yes, they needed to use the bathroom. Yes, they were hungry.

The man pointed. The boys shuffled off the platform and relieved themselves in the dry grass by the wall of the station. Memo kept close on one side of Samuele; Roberto kept close on the other. Soldiers walked among the boys handing them hunks of dense, sweet-smelling dark bread and shouting, *"Brot."* Other soldiers followed, each carrying a bucket of water and a tin cup: *"Wasser."* The boys drank fast.

Roberto scanned the crowd of older boys on the other side of the station. Was that Sergio? He waved.

A soldier came up and said something.

"I was just trying to see my brother."

The soldier hit him in the shoulder with the butt of his rifle.

Roberto let out a yelp. His *Brot* flew out of his hand. He staggered backward. He looked down. *Keep your mouth shut. Do what everyone else does. Keep your mouth shut. Do what everyone else does.*

The soldier shook his rifle threateningly at Roberto. Then he walked on.

Samuele picked up the *Brot* and handed it to Roberto without looking at him. But he touched him gently on the shoulder.

Roberto brushed the dirt off the *Brot*. He ate in big, greedy bites. His shoulder ached something awful. But the *Brot* was good. He could sink his teeth into it. He could chew and chew. He would think of nothing but the *Brot* filling the huge hole of his stomach. He blinked his burning eyes and ate. His nose ran. He wiped it with the back of his hand.

Soldiers shouted orders to the group of older boys now. They were being sorted by their city of origin—that much was easy to understand. Roberto saw Sergio take his place with the boys who had gotten on the train in Mestre. Then a soldier went by and picked one boy from each group and marched off with them, down the road. Another soldier did the same, always picking only one boy from each group.

"I'll go with the boys from Bolzano," said Memo. He looked at Samuele. "Enzo, you go with the boys from Trento. That way we can try to wind up in the same group, right?"

"Enzo?" said Roberto in confusion.

"What, did you forget my name?" Samuele looked at Roberto meaningfully; then he scratched his chest. "It's a good Catholic nickname."

Roberto blinked. He felt stupid, and that scared him worse. Of course he knew *Samuele* was a Jewish name. He just hadn't thought fast enough. He had to think fast. Much faster. Like Memo. He rubbed his shoulder where the rifle butt had hit him. He checked: Sergio still hadn't been chosen yet.

The soldiers shouted orders at the younger boys now. The group from Mestre and Venice was forming. Roberto's hand went to his Saint Christopher medal.

"Go on," whispered Memo. "When they pick you, I'll step to the front of my group and maybe they'll pick me, too. It's a good idea, right?"

Roberto watched Samuele nod. No, not Samuele—Enzo. Roberto had to think of him as Enzo from now on, so he wouldn't accidentally give him away. Roberto quickly unclasped the chain around his neck. He kissed the medal and handed it to Enzo. Then he ran to the Mestre–Venice group.

Only a Catholic boy would wear a Saint Christopher's medal. And Roberto would be okay without it. He'd be okay.

The groups from Padova, Verona, Trento, and Bolzano formed. Soldiers walked by, picking one boy from each group. Roberto tried to see what was happening with the bigger boys, but his view was blocked. He stepped to the front. A soldier gestured for him to come. Roberto walked behind him from group to group. He looked over at the bigger boys' groups. Sergio was gone.

Enzo was waiting at the front of the Trento group. The soldier picked him. Enzo took his place behind the soldier. He didn't look at Roberto. Roberto's chain showed at Enzo's neckline, with the medal hidden inside his shirt.

They walked on to the Bolzano group. Memo was standing at the front. The soldier picked the boy beside Memo.

Roberto swallowed the lump in his throat. He didn't dare look back over his shoulder as they walked away.

The soldier walked ahead of the five boys in Roberto's group through city block after city block. Morning had come, and the air was full of the sweet smells of baking. Motorcycles roared past them. Bicyclists crowded the streets. A group of children younger than Roberto—they were maybe ten or eleven—shouted at them and spat. They taunted with a single word, over and over: *Juden, Juden, Juden.*

The soldier called back. Something about *Italiener*—Italians.

The German children stopped their shouts. They ran on.

The group walked through the streets, and no one else, no one beyond the German children, said anything to them. No one acted as though there was anything odd about soldiers marching boys through the streets. In Venice everyone would have gawked. Soldiers shouldn't be bothering with children—someone should protest. Mamma would have protested. All the women of Cannaregio would have protested. Someone should speak for the boys.

Roberto remembered the boy on the train guessing that they were going to become soldiers. Maybe they were heading off to a training camp. Infantry or cavalry. Still, they shouldn't have just been taken like that. The more he breathed the fresh morning air, the more angry he became. Then the image of three boys lying in their own blood on the train platform blotted out the anger. The image seemed too grotesque to be real.

The soldier walked the group of five out of town and down a country road through woods. Roberto's stomach wouldn't stop growling. Memo would have laughed. Maybe. They came to an open area where trees had been cut down. Boys Roberto's age worked with picks and shovels.

The soldier led them to a truck at the edge of the clearing. He shouted at them. Enzo grabbed a pick out of the back of the truck. The soldier nodded and said something. Roberto grabbed a pick. The other three boys took picks.

They followed the soldier down the clearing to a section that hadn't been worked yet. The soldier pointed. The boys swung their picks.

The soldier watched for a while, his arms folded on his chest. Then he walked off to talk with another soldier.

One of the boys said something in a dialect Roberto couldn't understand.

Roberto spoke out of the side of his mouth, which

seemed to be the way all of them were speaking now. "It was stupid of them to mix boys from different towns. Now we can't speak to each other comfortably."

Enzo hissed, "Stupid like a fox."

"What do you mean?"

"If we can't talk like buddies—if we have to use school Italian with each other—then we can understand enough to work together, but we won't become buddies; we won't help each other." Enzo swung his pick hard. "We're lost."

Roberto gripped the handle of his pick tight. He wasn't lost; he had Enzo. He swung the pick. "What's the point of tilling a field out here? The soil's nothing but rocks."

"Be careful. They're looking at us."

Roberto snuck a glance over his shoulder. A different soldier watched them. Roberto turned his head down and swung with all his might. When he dared to peek again, the soldier had left. Roberto spoke without looking at Enzo and without pausing his pick. "It's stupid to till this rocky earth."

"Maybe it's not for planting."

So what were they digging? War trenches? The newsreels were full of war trenches. But who was going to fight a battle out here in these woods?

What else could they be digging?

Graves? Graves for the returned bodies of dead German soldiers. No, please, please don't let it be graves.

They picked and picked. The sun was hot. Roberto

panted. His tongue went dry as a withered pinecone. He thought of the rocking of a gondola, the rocking of a train. He picked in rhythm with that rocking.

One of the boys fell. He got up quickly. He said something about water.

Roberto needed water, too. He stopped for a moment and looked around. The shade of the woods beckoned. The fingers of both his hands were curled into claws, stiff from holding the same position for so long. He leaned the pick against his leg and stretched his fingers.

"Flexing for an attack?" said Enzo. "Forget it."

"What?"

"A pick against a gun," said Enzo, swinging his pick. "He'd shoot you before you got close enough. It won't work. Swing your pick, Roberto. Please. Swing it."

Roberto hadn't thought about matching his pick to a gun. It wasn't that at all. He'd thought simply about resting. Now he considered his pick as he swung. It could split a man's throat, if it was handled right. Nausea rose to Roberto's mouth. He swallowed. His throat hurt. His shoulder throbbed.

The first soldier came back. Through shouts and gestures, the boys understood to put down their picks. They followed him to the truck and sat on the ground near another group of boys. The soldier barked. They got up and sat again, farther away this time.

Each boy was given a boiled potato and a hunk of bread—*Brot*. They ate in silence. The soldiers came around with the familiar tin cup and water bucket.

Roberto heard a motor. Another army truck came up the road and parked in the clearing. Soldiers jumped out of the rear. The soldiers in charge of the boys talked with the new soldiers. Someone unfolded a map. Their voices rose in excitement. They pointed to places on the map.

The boy beside Roberto dropped sideways on the ground. His eyes shut. His potato rolled out of his hand.

A soldier glanced over at him. He shouted.

The boy didn't move.

The soldier walked toward them.

Roberto pinched the boy. "Sit up," he whispered.

The soldier shouted at Roberto.

Roberto looked down. He curled his shoulders to protect them from the rifle butt.

The soldier kicked the boy in the side.

The boy didn't flinch. And now Roberto was sure: The boy had fainted. Roberto pulled his knees up to his chest and wrapped his arms around his legs. *Keep your mouth shut. Do what everyone else does.*

The soldier kicked the boy again. His boots were thick and heavy. They could crush the boy's chest. The soldier stepped back for a harder kick.

Roberto couldn't stand it any longer. "He fainted."

The soldier shouted at Roberto. He grabbed him by the front of the shirt and pulled him to his feet. He pushed him toward the group of soldiers. He said something to them. Then he let go of Roberto and walked back to the boy who had fainted. He shot him.

Roberto clapped his hand over his mouth to hold in the scream. Someone pushed him against the back of the truck and shouted and slapped both his cheeks. Roberto was biting on his hand now, biting hard. The soldier shouted in his face and pulled his hand away from his mouth. It took Roberto a few seconds to focus, but he finally understood what the soldier wanted; he climbed into the back of the truck. He shut his eyes. Then he quickly opened them again. It was better to see everything and stay ready.

Another boy was pushed into the truck. He was big—his neck was thick and strong. A third climbed in. He was big, too. The boys glanced at one another, then looked away.

Two more boys climbed into the truck. The engine rumbled. Roberto was going somewhere else again. And this time he was going alone. Alone. The thought petrified him. His head swam.

Enzo climbed in. His eyes were ice. He didn't look at anyone. Vomit covered his chin and a trickle of blood ran down his temple, but he didn't seem to notice. He sat with his back straight in the middle of the truck bed. Roberto understood: Enzo had managed to get himself into the truck and that's all that mattered. Enzo had paid the passage in flesh—to keep them together.

Roberto vowed he would do the same. Whatever the cost, he'd stay with Enzo. They were a team. As long as they stayed together, they would be all right. They had to stay together.

Three soldiers got on. The truck rolled out of the clearing. They bumped their way down the country road.

WASSER

Roberto shielded his eyes from the glare of the sun and looked down the tarmac. He had worked here every day for a month, maybe longer, with Italian boys from all over the north of Italy. They had built this runway entirely by themselves, working side by side, mostly without talking. And when they did talk, it was usually to themselves. Everyone's home dialect was so different— especially the dialects of Bolzano and Venice—that communication was an effort, and no one seemed to want to try their common tongue: school Italian. It was as though they didn't believe they'd be there long enough to matter to each other. Or maybe each of them was looking out for himself—wary of sharing information.

They'd done a good job on the tarmac, in any case. They didn't know when the first plane would land, but Roberto was sure it would be soon because they'd been worked extra hard for the past two days. The soldiers' shouts had carried an element of frenzy. Now, finally, they were getting a rest.

Roberto walked over to the farmhouse and sat on the ground beside Enzo with his back against the wall. He had only a vague idea of where he was. Germany somewhere. Pretty far north and east and pretty far from anywhere, it seemed. He rubbed his hands together. They were calloused from holding the handle of a pick so tightly. The callouses weren't all that different from the callouses on his father's hands from holding the oar of the gondola all day. When Roberto was little, he used to trace his father's callouses with his index finger. And his father would tell him stories about feats with his gondola: how he had rowed as fast as he could from the banks known as the Zattere to the island of Giudecca for a groom who was late to his own wedding and how he'd rowed extra hard when a group of vagabond Australians working their way around the world had talked him into allowing all eight of them into the gondola at once for a ride the full length of the Canal Grande. Roberto put his hands to his cheeks and pretended for just a moment that his father's hands were cupping his face. His father was probably grasping the oar right now.

Roberto dropped his hands on the ground between his raised knees. The dirt was hard and dry. Everything was dry here. He missed the water of Venice. He missed the bright flowers that burst over the walls of hidden gardens. He missed the smell of the sea, the sting of salty wind in his face. He missed the food. Especially the food. Especially olives.

"Quack! Quack, quack, quack, quack." The duckling that had appeared on the farm just a few days ago chased the dog around the barn. Somehow it had taken to the mangy yellow dog, quacking in delight whenever the dog came by and racing after him. The dog obviously hated the bird. Every now and then he'd stop and snap at it. But the duckling just quacked and stretched tall, flapping its useless, tiny wings. And the dog would take off again, with the duck close behind.

Roberto smiled at them now.

Enzo reached in his pocket and pulled out a sausage— a wurst. He handed it to Roberto. Roberto gave him a boiled egg in return. The Germans gave them wurst every night and cheese or eggs every morning. Since Enzo didn't eat pork, he and Roberto exchanged. On the egg days, Roberto didn't mind. He'd never liked boiled eggs in the first place. But on the cheese days, it was hard. The cheese smelled good, and once he'd broken off a small piece and tasted it. It wasn't anything like the cheeses he knew at home, but it was pungent and rich.

Roberto wolfed down the wurst now. He was always hungry, despite the *Brot* and potato that came at every meal. The only thing that seemed to ease his hunger pang was sleep. But he wasn't sleepy now.

The rest of the boys were scattered in groups around the outbuildings of the farm. The soldiers used to watch them closely. But one of them got away somehow anyway. The next day a man and a woman returned him, his hands tied together with rope. They walked up to the farm with him and turned him over. The man and the woman had ordinary faces—they didn't look cruel. Good citizens doing their duty. That's when all the boys realized there was no point in running away.

The soldiers lined up the Italian boys side by side. The boys watched the soldiers pick up sticks and beat the boy who had run away. His black and blue marks had turned yellowish green by now, but Roberto knew they still hurt. The boy winced when anything brushed his back or legs.

Roberto ran his hands along his own calves now. They had no bruises. He rolled his shoulders backward a few times. No aches or pains. Nothing hurt him today but hunger and homesickness. And this was probably true of all the boys except the one who had run away, for the soldiers had been particularly lenient lately. No one had been beaten all week. In fact, the soldiers had been letting them do whatever they wanted when it was break time from work. They were clearly buoyed up by the German successes.

One of them had tried to explain to the boys. He'd

drawn a map in the dirt and pointed and gestured and re-peated, over and over, until they got the gist of it. German forces had invaded Egypt—and they were obviously doing well, much better than Italy had done there almost two years ago now. Next they'd moved ahead in their invasion of Russia. They had taken a town called Sevastopol on the Black Sea. The Soviets had piled up bags of sand to hide behind when the bullets flew. But the sand saved no one. The soldier laughed. The war would be over soon; victory was within reach. He gave the news as though the boys should rejoice in their common victory.

And the boys did rejoice. Roberto, too. He couldn't wait. But not because he cared about winning. Instead, it was because victory meant he'd see his mother and father. And Sergio and Memo. Victory meant he'd go home.

Roberto leaned toward Enzo. "What do you think our job will be now that the tarmac's built?"

Enzo finished his egg. He looked off. It was clear he wasn't going to answer. He talked less and less these days. Partly that was to keep the soldiers from noticing their friendship and maybe splitting them up. But even when no one was watching, Enzo hardly talked. Except at night. If something awful had happened during the day, Roberto would have trouble falling asleep. So Enzo would tell him stories to put him to sleep. Just like Roberto's father used to tell him stories.

Enzo stretched his arms out in front now and yawned. His upper arms were thick with muscles.

Roberto rubbed his own thickening arms. "I hope it's outside work again. I like feeling strong."

"We're not good for anything else." Enzo slid his butt out from the wall till he was lying flat. He closed his eyes.

"This is the longest break we've had."

Enzo yawned again and rolled on his side.

At night the boys slept in the barn. They stretched out where they could, fighting for the straw. Only Roberto and Enzo didn't fight. Enzo said he couldn't afford to have any-one dislike him. And Roberto wasn't a fighter, anyway. So the two of them slept on earth packed hard by hooves. Roberto sometimes woke in the night because Enzo tossed and turned. Enzo slept badly. He needed this catnap now. Roberto leaned his head back against the wall and looked at the sky. It was nearly cloudless, bright and clean. You wouldn't know bombs were falling in Germany or Egypt or Russia or anywhere. The sky seemed serene.

The soldier they called Wasser, because he was the one who usually came around with the water bucket, stood at the foot of the tarmac and blew his whistle. Roberto shook Enzo by the shoulder. They joined the other boys in line.

Wasser said something about water. He waved his arms. Then he laughed. Wasser liked to laugh. None of the boys joined in. Ever. But that didn't stop Wasser. He chuckled

to himself and marched off across a harvested field, calling for them to follow. They walked through a second field
and into a stand of trees.

"One against eighteen," whispered Enzo in Roberto's
ear.

Roberto didn't answer, and he knew Enzo didn't expect
him to. Even though the Germans treated the boys like
prisoners, they were technically a work force under German control. Italy and Germany were together in this war,
after all. They were fascists together.

And if Roberto forgot about that alliance and really let
himself think about fighting Wasser and the other soldiers,
as though the Germans were the enemy, there still wasn't
any point in answering Enzo. Enzo knew as well as anyone
that it was eighteen against a whole country. Everyone remembered the man and woman who had brought back the
runaway.

Enzo wouldn't do anything rash; he just said things—
things he never intended to do. Roberto remembered Enzo
talking about the soldiers on the train car—"two of them
to a whole carload of us"—and he remembered how Enzo
had thought of the picks as weapons when Roberto had
never even considered such a thing—and he could think
of at least a dozen other times Enzo had whispered words
of rebellion, tallying up the odds. That was just Enzo's way.
Fighting words. Roberto liked it when Enzo said those

things because at least he was talking; at least Roberto could hear a voice other than his own that he understood without effort.

They came out of the trees at the edge of a stream. Wasser said something that, for once, wasn't an order. He spoke in an almost friendly tone. He made a gesture like he was diving.

The boys unbuttoned their clothes. Within moments some of them were stripped and wading in.

Roberto looked quickly at Enzo, his cheeks hot with alarm. Enzo stared straight ahead and walked to the edge of the water, almost as though he were marching. He stripped off his shirt.

Roberto stripped off his own grimy shirt. He'd lived in these clothes ever since they'd left Venice. It was a relief to be free of them. He could tell from their faces that everyone felt the same way. The boys in the water splashed each other and actually laughed. It would have been a wonderful moment—clean and free—if it weren't for the worry. Roberto moved closer to Enzo.

Enzo sat and took off his shoes. Then he pulled off his shorts and underwear together, still sitting. His privates were hidden between his legs. Roberto did the same. They ran into the water, Enzo half hunched over, splashing at Roberto. Roberto splashed back. He tried to smile. He tried to pretend they were having fun.

And now they were up to their waists in water, safe at last. They swam. Closer and closer to the other side. For a second, only a second, the thought of escape flashed through Roberto's head. Futile thought. There was nowhere to escape to.

Wasser shouted.

Roberto and Enzo swam back toward the first side. One of the boys called to them. He said something in an Alpine dialect—and Roberto figured out it was about how well they swam. The boy's voice was full of surprise. Roberto looked around. Only three other boys were swimming besides him and Enzo. Any Venetian boy knew how to swim. But someone from an inland village, a hamlet in the mountains, where would he learn to swim unless he lived on a lake or a river? Roberto panicked for a second. Could anyone there possibly remember that at the train station in Munich, Enzo had lined up with the boys from Trento? Was there a river near Trento? A lake? Roberto couldn't think of any from his school geography lessons. Some of these boys had been with Roberto and Enzo since that train ride, but surely they'd been thinking about their own worries. They couldn't remember who had lined up where. No one could remember that. And even if they did, what would it matter? So a boy from Trento knew how to swim. So what?

Still, Roberto came back into the shallow water. He

drank. The stream was delicious. He turned to tell Enzo how good the water tasted, but Enzo wasn't behind him. Enzo still swam in the middle. He swam in circles like a goldfish in a bowl. He swam and swam and swam.

Wasser blew his whistle. The other boys got out of the water and shook off, doglike. Still wet, they put their clothes on.

Enzo still swam.

Wasser shouted to him.

Roberto stood in knee-deep water and watched Enzo. His heart beat so hard his chest moved up and down. All eyes were on Enzo, eyes that they had tried so hard to hide from up till now. If people kept watching, they would see Enzo as he got out of the water—they would know he was Jewish. Roberto should do something. Anything. But he couldn't move. He felt glued to the spot. Numb with doom.

Wasser's face turned red. He blew his whistle hard. The blood vessels in his forehead stood out.

Roberto turned to him suddenly, his head buzzing. "He can't hear well," he said loudly. He hit his ears with the palms of his hands. "He's sort of deaf." Roberto didn't wait for an answer. He swam out, desperation driving his arms and legs faster and faster. He grabbed Enzo by the elbow, not knowing what to expect, ready to punch him if that's what it took.

Enzo turned his head toward Roberto with a dreamy

smile. It was as though he didn't understand anything, as though the wild fear in Roberto was part of another world. He let Roberto pull him back into the shallow water easily.

Everyone watched. Wasser's brows tightened, and his face was hard. Roberto knew he had been stupid to say Enzo was deaf. Everyone knew Enzo wasn't deaf. Roberto had been stupid stupid stupid, and now they would both pay. But Wasser gave a quick, firm nod. He pointed to the shore and said something. Then he walked to the edge of the wood and blew the whistle.

The boys hurried to line up.

Roberto came out of the water slowly, with Enzo close behind and off to the side away from the other boys.

"Didn't you love it?" whispered Enzo. "For a little while I pretended I was home."

"Love it?" Roberto almost choked on the words. "That was crazy." He spoke out of the side of his mouth. The fear was subsiding, and a new sharp feeling seared his eyes. He blinked hard as he sat and pulled on his clothes.

"It wasn't crazy. It was fun."

"It was as crazy as when you walked to the end of the train car and Memo and I had to rescue you." Roberto's fingers fumbled on his buttons, he was so angry now. He remembered what Memo had said in the train—he told Enzo he wouldn't follow him the next time he did something stupid. Maybe Roberto shouldn't follow Enzo next time. "Don't do those things."

"Why not? What could be a better place for it than water?"

"A better place for what?"

Enzo looked at Roberto. Then he looked away. "It doesn't matter. You're right."

What didn't matter? Roberto stood up. There was something terrible in what Enzo said—something in the tone of it—something too terrible to think about. Roberto's anger vanished. "Whatever you do, I'll be there. You won't be alone. Ever." His voice caught. "You'll get us both in trouble."

Enzo stood up, too. "You will, won't you? You'll be there." He took a deep breath. "I'm sorry, Roberto. I won't do it again."

A boy knocked into Enzo from behind. Roberto hadn't realized anyone was nearby. This boy was one of the few who had been swimming. He looked at them as he passed. And there was something in his eyes, in the set of his jaw. In an instant, Roberto understood this boy knew Enzo's secret. Roberto went numb, all over again.

Enzo didn't even look at Roberto, though Roberto was sure that Enzo, too, had seen the message in the boy's face. Instead, Enzo walked quickly to the line. Roberto followed, moving without thought, as though in a nightmare.

That night the nameless boy came up behind Enzo at dinner. He tapped Enzo on the shoulder. He held out his hand. Enzo gave him his wurst. Roberto sucked in air. That was supposed to be Roberto's wurst. The boy stuck the wurst in his pocket and held his hand out again. Enzo hesitated. The boy waited. Enzo gave him his potato. The boy went off and sat down to eat.

Roberto's head spun. The wurst was gone. Enzo's potato was gone. Just gone. And it was so long till breakfast. Roberto looked at his own food. He was hungry. Viciously hungry. He split his potato and handed half to Enzo. Enzo took it without a word.

Roberto offered him half his wurst. Enzo shook his head. Roberto wanted to argue, though his fingers stayed closed possessively around the wurst. How could Enzo stick to his food restrictions when there was so little to eat? Roberto hadn't thought twice about not eating wurst on Friday, even though he was Catholic and he wasn't supposed to eat meat on Friday. He didn't even know what day was what by now, but he knew that he'd eaten wurst on at least three Fridays since he'd come to Germany, maybe four, maybe five—and he didn't care. Oh, he did, of course he cared—but he didn't suffer over it. He wouldn't let himself. God would understand. If anyone should understand, God should. "God would want us to stay strong," he said to Enzo.

Enzo took a bite of potato. "God wants me to know who I am. Especially now." Enzo took another bite. "And I do. If I was starving, I'd have to eat it. That's the Hebrew admonition of *pekuach nefesh*—saving a life is the most important thing. But I'm not starving. Not yet."

Roberto's stomach growled. He refused to listen to it. He held out the other half of the potato.

Enzo looked away and shook his head. "No, thanks."

Roberto shoved the potato into Enzo's hand and went off to eat his *Brot* and wurst by himself. He chewed extra long. He tried to think about how thick and good this *Brot* was. Instead, he heard stomping feet on a giant drum, the hollow drum of his stomach. He squeezed his eyes shut and willed himself to feel again the cool, pure water of the stream this afternoon. Instead, the agony of watching Enzo swim jabbed his empty gut.

He went to sleep early.

BARBED WIRE

A plane landed in the middle of the night. Roberto heard the engine and then the confusion outside. He sat up.

"Go back to sleep," said Enzo. "If there's work to do, they'll wake us soon enough."

Roberto rolled on his side. He listened hard to try to catch the tone of the voices. He still knew almost no German words, but he had learned he could tell a lot about how he was going to be treated from the soldiers' tone of voice. He scratched his arm and listened to them now.

"Once upon a time there was a hunchback boy." Enzo's voice was low and mellow. His face was right beside Roberto's. "Everyone made fun of him. They tortured him. They kicked him and threw filth on the back of his pants so people would think he couldn't control his bowels. So he ran away." Enzo spoke very slowly. Roberto could tell he was sleepy. "He dug a deep hole that slanted sideways, so that when he crawled into it, it formed a roof over his head. He lined it with smooth stones from the beach. It was his cave—his own handmade cave." Enzo's voice was so tired. He needed sleep desperately. But Roberto knew Enzo would keep talking until he was sure Roberto was asleep.

Roberto lay on his back as still as he could. He concentrated on breathing rhythmically and loudly, like a person sleeping. And, as he'd expected, Enzo soon stopped talking and fell into his own deep sleep.

The first night in this work camp, when Roberto couldn't sleep because the image of the soldier shooting the boy who had fainted kept replaying in his head, Enzo told him Bible stories from the times before Christ. He said his family told each other these stories to keep their spirits strong when things went bad. The next night he told another story. And the night after that. Roberto looked forward to them. He counted on them. He asked for the best ones over and over.

Later, Enzo moved on to stories he made up himself. He'd work in details from their day—but he'd twist them so that they came out magical, so that the boys in the stories always wound up safe. This story about the hunchback boy was promising. Roberto wanted to hear the rest of that story. He would have to ask Enzo to repeat it another night.

Roberto stared through the dark at the underside of the loft above. His stomach contracted into a small, hard ball. He listened to the sleep noises of the other boys. He listened to the rustles of rats in the straw. He listened to the rise and fall of voices outside, sometimes close, sometimes far away. Their tarmac was being used. They were part of the war.

Roberto had played war as a kid—when he was seven and eight. And he had gone to some of the drills in the *campo*s in Venice, where everyone told stories about people they knew who'd been in wars. But none of the play and none of the talk had ever been like this. It had been heroic. In the war games, Roberto had triumphed over evil. In the stories about battles, Italians had won with their ferocity and honor. But here what Roberto did amounted to working like a slave, under shouts he couldn't understand, without enough food.

Roberto made fists of both hands and pressed them against his growling stomach. He remembered Sergio punching him in the belly last winter, punching him hard again and again. It was right after Memo's thirteenth birthday. Memo had decided it was time to learn how to drink something more than just wine. So he'd gotten a small bottle of grappa, and he and Roberto had finished it off together. Roberto had never been so sick in his life—and he'd never been sick without being able to tell Mamma. Sergio had punched him to make him vomit. It worked. But Roberto always suspected that Sergio hadn't done it just to help.

Sergio and Memo. They could take care of themselves. They were fine. Maybe they were even back in Venice by now. Both of them knew how to fend for themselves better than Roberto ever had. Roberto pounded his fists on his stomach. Sergio and Memo were fine. He pounded rhythmically. They were fine, fine, fine, fine.

Roberto let his hands drop to his sides. He said his good-night prayers again and waited for sleep. He waited and waited.

Dawn came at last, and with it the shrill of Wasser's whistle. Roberto got up and ran for breakfast. He was close to the front of the line. His hands itched with the need to grab the food.

This morning was cheese. Roberto put his potato, *Brot*, and cheese in his pocket. He looked around. There was Enzo, halfway back in the line. The nameless boy was behind him. Roberto stood unmoving. He watched the line move forward. Enzo took his food and stepped out of line. The boy got his food; then he followed Enzo. He tapped him on the shoulder. Enzo handed over his potato and cheese in one move. Beautiful potato. Beautiful, beautiful cheese.

Roberto stared at Enzo, who was standing alone now.

They were hungry enough as it was. And now they had half as much as before, except for the *Brot*. At least the thief didn't take Enzo's *Brot*. Maybe he was half decent. Or maybe he didn't like the black German loaves.

Roberto walked over to Enzo and handed him the potato. "Eat half and I'll eat half and we can trade." He took a bite of the cheese. This was the first time he'd be able to eat the cheese, since he wouldn't be trading Enzo for his wurst anymore. That was one way to look at the new development: At least now he could have a half portion of cheese every other day. And it was such good cheese.

Enzo ate half the potato and passed it to Roberto. "I'm not hungry. You finish the cheese."

Roberto put the cheese in Enzo's hand. "Eat it. You'd do the same for me. And I need you alive or I'll forget how to talk."

Enzo gave a small laugh. He ate the cheese.

The soldier they called Arbeiter, because he was always using that word when he urged them through their jobs, shouted to them to assemble. There were mounds of barbed wire on the ground. Arbeiter shouted and gestured. They understood: Their job today was to build an enclosure. They cut down saplings for the supports and lopped off the branches till they had smooth poles. They dug deep holes and stood the poles in them. They wedged in rocks to hold the poles steady, with dirt packed into every crevice. They ran the wire from pole to pole, only a few inches off the ground. Then they ran another line of wire a hand's width above the first. Then another and another, as high as they could reach. It had to be an animal pen out here in the field—maybe for horses. Nothing else would need so high a fence. Or maybe the soldiers wanted to keep people out. Maybe they were going to protect something in the pen.

They finished by early afternoon. Then they drank water and sat in the shade. The water didn't satisfy, though. The rumblings of Roberto's stomach got louder. He looked around. The thief sat off alone, his legs crossed. He played with something in the dirt. He wasn't hungry. He was full, on stolen food. And he'd steal again. And Enzo would let him. And for what? Indignation stirred in Roberto. "What would happen if they found out about you?" He nudged Enzo. "What would happen, anyway?"

Enzo sucked in his bottom lip. "Maybe they'd put me in a camp with other Jews."

"Oh, yeah. I read about the Jewish work camps in the newspaper. They're probably just like this."

"They're a lot worse."

Roberto scratched his cheek. "How?"

"I don't know."

But there was something about the way he said it—he did know. "Tell me."

"My father heard that they kill people in some of the camps."

"Well, I know that. Hitler said himself that when workers get so sick that their life is nothing more than suffering, he puts them to death."

"Maybe in some camps, but not in these. Everyone sent to these camps dies."

Roberto pulled at his brows in confusion. "Camps just for sick people?"

"No. For all kinds of people."

Roberto swallowed. "So why do they kill them then?"

"Because they're Jews, of course."

"They can't kill someone just for being Jewish."

"Listen to yourself." Enzo's voice grew hoarse. "Your insomnia—my nightmares—they don't come from nowhere. They killed the boys on the train just for wanting to go home. They killed that boy at the first work camp just for fainting."

Roberto's nose stung. He blinked his eyes. He'd been keeping Enzo's secret all along. It had been a challenge, a responsibility. It had been important. But it hadn't been dire. He'd never allowed himself to think about what was really at stake. Not even yesterday, when Enzo said, "What could be a better place for it than water?" That horrifying, unspecified "it."

Roberto shook his head now. He wouldn't believe Enzo's

words. He couldn't. "My father brings home the newspaper every day. There was nothing in them about killing healthy Jews."

"Some news doesn't get printed."

"But something like that, people would know. People would talk about it."

"Jews talk about it." Enzo rubbed his nose and looked away. "It hasn't been going on all that long. It started this spring. Death camps. They're in Poland, I think." The words came with slow deliberateness. Totally matter of fact, as though they weren't the worst words in the world. "Jews are moved from the work camps to the death camps. There's a work camp near Munich." Enzo looked back at Roberto. "When our train pulled up to the Munich station, I figured I'd die there." Enzo's voice held the same tone it had when he came out of the water yesterday—the tone that was so terrible. The tone of resignation.

A wall crumbled inside Roberto's heart. It was true. He moved closer to Enzo, so that they sat with their shoulders touching. "We don't have any death camps in Italy, do we?"

"No. Not yet, anyway." Then Enzo shook his head. "I'm sorry I said that. I bet there will never be any in Italy."

Roberto pulled a piece of straw out from the dirt that encrusted it. He picked at it, flicking the dirt away. He breathed heavily. He was facing the road that led up to the farm. That's why he was one of the first to see them arrive. There must have been fifty or more. Men and women and children. They walked as though they were machines, as though they'd been walking forever and could keep walking forever. They looked nowhere. They said nothing. A crowd of silent people—even the children. Soldiers walked on both sides and in the front and back. Roberto didn't know why the soldiers bothered. These people weren't capable of running away. He could tell from the slump of their shoulders. He could tell from the listless drop of their feet.

The people were herded into the pen. They didn't mill around. They found a spot and sat immediately, clustered in little groups. Roberto studied them. Family groups. So many families in a pen.

So many bare feet.

So many bones under dry skin.

A soldier shouted. Roberto found himself pushed backward. He realized he had gotten up and walked over to the enclosure. He'd been standing outside, staring in. The soldier yelled at him. He pointed at the people in the pen. He said the same word over and over, a word Roberto had heard before: *Juden*. Where? He remembered now—it was the word the German children had shouted when the soldier had marched his small troop of five boys through the streets of Munich.

Roberto turned around and walked to the closest farm building. He sat down with his back against the wall. He pulled up his knees and looked at his feet. Those people were nothing to him. He didn't know who they were. He didn't know what they had done. He wouldn't guess at it. No! They had nothing to do with him. Nothing. His stomach growled. He had problems of his own.

That afternoon, the boys started building a low wooden storage shed near the landing strip. Roberto didn't know what it was for, and he didn't want to know. He swung his ax as rhythmically as he had swung the pick. At dusk the boys lined up for *Brot*, wurst, and potato. Enzo handed his wurst and potato over to the thief. Then Roberto and Enzo went off behind the chicken coop to eat.

The people in the pen were being given food now, too. *Brot* and *Wasser*. Roberto waited. Where were the potato and wurst? The people ate their food, jaws moving distinctly under the tight flesh of hollow cheeks. Roberto looked at his own food. Those people were nothing to him. He handed Enzo the potato, and he took a bite of wurst.

A girl in the pen looked out at Roberto. Her eyes were black. Her hair was stringy and dirty. Her face was unforgiving. She was older than him. Maybe Sergio's age. A smaller girl sat on her lap. They were so thin, Roberto felt sure he could circle the girl's arm with his thumb and index finger.

Roberto still had a few bites of wurst left. He turned his back on the girl and ate quickly. This was his food. This was his life.

Enzo got up and walked off without a word. Roberto watched him turn the corner of the barn.

In the morning Roberto and Enzo shared food behind the chicken coop again. They sat on the ground in the shade. Roberto didn't mean to look over at the people in the pen. But he did. They were eating *Brot*. And the girl was looking at him. He looked away immediately.

"They're Polish Jews." Enzo finished his half of the egg and handed the rest over to Roberto.

"How do you know?"

"I listened to the soldiers. They said 'Polnisch.' They said 'Juden.' Some words are the same in any language."

There was that word Roberto had heard. But it was so different from *ebrei*, the Italian word for "Jews." "How did you know *Juden* meant 'Jews'?"

"*Judea* was the name of an ancient land of my people. You know that."

Roberto felt foolish for not making the connection— after all, so many of Enzo's nighttime stories had taken place in Judea. And, worse, he felt frightened. He'd thought of himself as being more aware these days, more able to take care of himself. But if he failed to make such an obvious connection, he was still the same old Roberto—the boy with his head in the clouds, as Sergio said. He had to act smarter. "What are they doing here?"

"Waiting. It's a holding pen."

Roberto went cold. He wouldn't ask what for. He

wouldn't ask where they were going next. He didn't know anything about these people, really—where they had come from or how they got here. It didn't matter to him where they were going next. It couldn't matter to him. What could he do about it anyway?

The yellow dog barked and ran past with the duckling flapping and hopping after it.

The girl's sister squealed in delight at the sight. She ran to the barbed wire and grabbed it with both hands. Roberto gasped. But the little girl was lucky; she'd grabbed between the barbs. She shouted out happy words to the dog and duckling.

Roberto half smiled. The child was pitifully skinny and her dress was nothing but rags, yet she was happy at this moment. He stood up. He would catch the duckling—he would bring it over for her to pet.

Arbeiter stood a few meters down. He stepped up to the fence and took the wire that the girl held on to. He plucked it—like a musician plucks the string of a violin. Just one quick pluck. The wire bobbled and a barb hit the little girl in the face. She screamed as it ripped her lips. Blood ran down her neck and over her dress. Her sister grabbed her from behind and cradled her.

Roberto's whole body tensed. Enzo jumped to his feet and held him by the elbow. "We can't help them, Roberto. We can't even help ourselves."

But Roberto didn't need Enzo's hand to hold him back.

Roberto wasn't about to go anywhere or do anything. There was nothing he could do.

His head felt hot and full. It would burst. He looked at the half egg in his hand. He had already finished his *Brot* and his half of potato, but this half egg remained. And now he found he was doing something, after all. Oh, yes, there was something he could do. He shook Enzo off and walked over to the enclosure. He reached his arm through the wires. "Here," he said to the big girl.

She grabbed the half egg and hid it in the folds of her skirt. Her movement was like a snake striking, so fast it was as though it had never happened. Roberto didn't realize someone who looked as lethargic as she did could move so fast. Her mouth was open, but she didn't say anything to him. She turned her head and crooned to the little girl on her lap.

Roberto stepped back. He expected a rifle butt in the shoulder or a whipping on his legs. Or worse. But nothing happened. He looked around. The soldiers talked in pairs here and there. The boys ate or waited in small groups. Only Enzo looked at him. Only Enzo had seen. If Roberto had tried to do it surreptitiously, he'd have been caught for sure. But he hadn't even tried to hide. It was like when Enzo had stepped up to the stream yesterday and undressed like everyone else. If a person moved as though he knew what he was doing, as though he were doing only things he had a right to do, he didn't draw attention. It was as though he became invisible.

Roberto felt a sudden sense of power. And something else—he was almost happy.

They spent the day finishing off the shed. Around dinnertime, three trucks rumbled up the road. The backs were loaded with boxes of ammunition. The drivers got out and talked with the soldiers in charge of the boys.

The boys lined up for dinner as usual. Roberto pocketed his wurst and handed his potato to Enzo. Then he walked over to the pen. The girl saw him coming. She moved closer to the wire. He held out the wurst. She snatched it and slid it into her clothes. It was an admission: She knew she was starving. She knew her sister was starving. Roberto walked on to the chicken coop as though nothing had happened.

Enzo was behind him. "Here." He handed Roberto the potato. "Give her this, too."

"Then you'll have nothing to eat but *Brot*."

"You have nothing but *Brot*."

Roberto shook his head. It was one thing to give the girl his own food; it was another to give her Enzo's food.

Enzo moved so close that his breath touched Roberto's cheek. "They're my people."

Roberto shook his head again.

Enzo hung his head. His mouth hardly moved as he

talked. "I wanted to help from the first moment I saw them, but I didn't know what to do. You did." He sighed. "Listen, I have to help now. I need to. But if I get caught giving food, they might find out I'm a Jew. They would kill me for sure. Then I wouldn't be any good to anyone." He pressed his lips together. "If you get caught, you might still live. I'm not saying you should do it. I don't think you should risk it. I wish you wouldn't." He looked into Roberto's eyes. "But as long as you're going to anyway, give her this potato." Enzo pressed the potato into Roberto's hand. "Let me help. Please."

Roberto took the potato. He walked back toward the pen. A soldier said something to him. Roberto stepped closer to the pen. The girl was within arm's length now, but she didn't look at him. The soldier watched. Roberto spat on the girl. The soldier still watched impassively; then he glanced away. Roberto gave the girl the potato. It disappeared into her clothes.

He walked back to Enzo. "How much do you love eggs?"

Enzo looked at Roberto as though he were crazy.

Roberto grinned. He felt reckless and as crazy as Enzo's eyes said he was, and, yes, there was that feeling again— he was almost happy. He walked into the chicken coop. The chickens sat on shelves, roosting in smelly heat. The sun came in through the wires that covered the high, glass-less windows. As he walked in, small feathers puffed out from under his feet. He stifled a sneeze. He reached under the closest hen. He took two eggs in one grab. The hen squawked and pecked at the top of his hand. He reached under another hen and took two more. He walked out.

Enzo was sitting on the ground, eating his *Brot* as though nothing special was going on.

Roberto handed him two eggs. "Ever eaten a raw egg?"

A sick look crossed Enzo's face, but he put one egg on the ground and held the other with both hands. "That's the best way. I've heard that's what they do in all the finest restaurants." He jammed his thumb down on the fatter end of the egg. A piece of shell broke off. Enzo looked at Roberto and smiled. Then he put the egg to his mouth and sucked.

Roberto did the same. He had eaten raw eggs at his cousins' home in the country, and he liked them. He could see the eggs disgusted Enzo, though, despite his smile. Maybe Jews didn't eat raw eggs much. But at least the religion didn't seem to prohibit it.

They both ate their second egg. Then they went off to the barn and lay there in the light of early evening, waiting for sleep.

Roberto rolled on his side. "What else can we eat around this farm?"

Enzo's eyes got a mischevious glint. "There's always the duckling."

"Raw? That's disgusting."

Enzo laughed. "What about the dog?"

"You're really demented."

Enzo laughed harder. And now he looked positively wicked. "What about . . ."

"Stop. Whatever it is, I don't want to hear it."

Enzo guffawed. Then he put his hands behind his neck and smiled up at the sky. "Roberto, you're so wonderfully easy to tease. I'm lucky to be here with you."

Lucky to be here. Lucky. Roberto was stunned. "Listen to what you just said."

"I know." Enzo was silent for a while. Then he spoke very softly. "The words just came out of me. But they're true. We'll keep the girl and her sister alive. We have that privilege. We have something worth doing at last." He whispered into Roberto's ear, "We can do it."

Roberto let himself roll onto his back. Evening was just beginning. The first stars showed in the pale blue. The heavens were in their place. "Tell me that story about the hunchback again."

"You mean the boy who sprouted wings?"

He sprouted wings? How perfect. "Yes, that one. Tell it exactly the same way."

STONES

The girl seemed to develop some sixth sense, for she always knew precisely when Roberto was coming with food. She positioned herself in a different spot every time, close to the wires but sometimes near one pole, sometimes midway between poles, sometimes near another pole. That was smart. That way the soldier on guard was less likely to recognize that it was the same girl Roberto walked up to twice a day.

And she usually came without her sister. She'd put the girl on some woman's lap or she'd set her to digging a hole with her bare fingers or she'd sit her down beside another small child. That was smart, too. The little girl was maybe old enough to figure out that Roberto was the source of the food, but not old enough to be counted on to know how not to give away a secret with her eyes or hands or body.

And Roberto did his own smart things. He made sure he went over to the pen at other times than just when he was giving the girl food. He walked by and stood with both hands in his pockets for a moment before breakfast and again before dinner. He found a few stones around the size of eggs and put them in his pockets. He took them out and rubbed them when he knew a soldier was watching. That way anyone who saw him with food in his pocket would think he just had those stones. He was acting almost clever. Memo would have been proud of him. Enzo was. Enzo told him he was smarter and braver than anyone else he'd ever known. It couldn't be true—but it made Roberto feel good anyway.

Roberto wasn't sure, but he thought he'd been feeding the girl for more than a week. She looked stronger, maybe, despite the fact that she slept on the ground in the pen. Her sister looked stronger, too. The little girl's lips were no longer swollen and red, though the scabs hadn't fallen off yet. And neither of them had been beaten, so far as he knew. Beatings of the Jews were erratic and random. The girl and her sister had been lucky.

And Enzo seemed to have grown accustomed to eating the raw eggs. He still didn't like them and he assumed that Roberto didn't like them, either, so he worked hard to make eating them a kind of game. He'd tell Roberto to concentrate and listen closely—and then he'd describe a wondrous feast, and they'd eat fast while the vision was fresh in their heads. Enzo ate two raw eggs at breakfast and two more at dinner. Roberto did the same. It wasn't a bad arrangement. Roberto, Enzo, the girl, her little sister—no one was starving.

Enzo seemed to thrive on it, despite his disgust. He just kept moving in stride, even last night, when Roberto had made the mistake of taking eggs out of nests on the top shelf of the chicken coop. Roberto worried that if he took from the same nests all the time, the farmer might notice that that hen wasn't laying as many as she used to. So he was careful to take from different nests. He had already taken from every nest on the middle and bottom shelves. That's why he started on the top shelf.

Roberto and Enzo cracked the eggs open last night, only to find tiny chicks curled up, just days from hatching. Enzo popped a chick into his mouth whole and chewed hard, his lips pressed together tight. Roberto wanted to do the same, but even with his eyes closed, he couldn't bring himself to put a chick in his mouth. To Roberto the difference between a raw egg and a raw chick was the difference between the sun and the moon. But to Enzo they were equally disgusting. So Enzo ate all three of them, spitting out the tiny beaks and feet.

At breakfast the next morning, this morning, Roberto was careful to pick from nests on the middle shelf. He would never raid a nest on the top shelf again.

Roberto wondered now if the formed chicks somehow held more nutrition than fresh eggs because Enzo seemed to work even better today than usual. Oh, Roberto and Enzo were the two hardest workers among the boys, no matter what the job was. They cut more wood; they dug deeper holes; they swung picks without slowing hour after hour, day after day. But right now Enzo walked ahead of Roberto faster and stronger than Roberto had ever seen him, as though nothing could tire him out. They carried boxes from the trucks that had rolled in yesterday afternoon over to the shed the boys had built. Tonight or maybe tomorrow night a plane would come and they would load the boxes from the shed onto the plane. They had finished the first truck's load and made decent headway on the others.

Arbeiter shouted and the boys lined up to be dismissed for a short break. The sun was high. Shade would be welcome.

For no reason, Roberto looked over at the pen. A few of the people were walking around. The girl was one of them. And she was looking right at him. When their eyes met, she straightened her ripped shirt, so that it covered her properly. Her modesty made his cheeks hot and his throat hurt. He was ashamed, ashamed for all these German soldiers, ashamed for himself.

The girl walked up to the wires and stooped down. Then she walked away without a glance backward.

Roberto went over to where she'd stooped. He picked up a stone. It was flat on one side and rounded on the other. Like a hemisphere. It was completely free of dirt in all its little fissures, as though someone had painstakingly cleaned it.

A heavy hand landed on Roberto's shoulder. He jumped around. Arbeiter said something to him. He took the stone from Roberto and turned it over in his hand. He said something again. Quick and to the point—whatever it was, Roberto knew looking at the ground wouldn't get him out of this one. Oh, please, let Arbeiter not have seen the girl put the stone there. Oh, please, please. Let it only be Roberto who was in trouble.

Roberto reached into his pocket and pulled out another stone. He handed it to Arbeiter. He said, "It's my collection." None of the soldiers had ever given any indication that they understood Italian, but maybe that was just an act, to fool the boys into saying dangerous things. Roberto took a third stone out of his other pocket. He pointed to a discoloration on one side of it. "See, if I knew anything about rocks, I could tell you what that was there. But I don't know anything. I just collect them because I need to. If you were me, you'd collect something, too. It helps."

Arbeiter just looked at the discolored stone.

Roberto dared to take the girl's stone from Arbeiter's hand. He replaced it quickly with the discolored stone. He held up the girl's stone in front of Arbeiter's nose. "It's flat on one side as though it's only half of something. Only half. I like it, don't you?" He kept an easy tone. Maybe he could soothe his way to safety. He thought of Arbeiter plucking the barbed wire when the little girl was holding tight. It happened so fast, Arbeiter couldn't have planned it. Cruelty was instinctive with him. There was no way anyone could soothe Arbeiter. Roberto tensed up to be ready to take whatever penalty might come. "It's just a collection." He spoke without emotion, though the tears pressed inside his eyes.

Arbeiter looked at Roberto. He held the two egg-shaped stones in one hand and picked his teeth with the other. Then, with one hard, fast move, he threw the stones at the people in the pen. One smacked the dirt. The other hit a woman on the shoulder. She fell forward on her hands and knees. Something rolled from her skirt. A man snatched it up and stuck it in his mouth as he stumbled away. Arbeiter said, *"Tier,"* and walked off.

Roberto stood stock-still, his heart beating violently. He watched the woman move slowly to a sitting position. She kept her eyes on the ground and she didn't stand up. But he told himself it was because she didn't want to. She was resting. With one hand she smoothed her hair—newly graying hair, like Roberto's mother's hair. Slowly she lifted her chin. Slowly, slowly her hand moved again and again on her hair, with a deliberation that made Roberto want to scream.

Just scream and scream and scream. He looked away. He didn't want her to see him watching. The tears behind his eyes had disappeared, leaving a burning dryness.

It was a piece of *Brot* that had rolled from the woman's skirt; Roberto was sure of that. That's why she never looked up to see who had taken it. Anyone could have. Anyone would have. They were starving.

Roberto slipped the girl's gift stone into his pocket and squeezed it as hard as he could.

At dinner Roberto gave the girl his potato and wurst. He was too hungry to wait, so he ate his *Brot* standing up halfway between the chicken coop and the pen. Enzo was already sitting by the chicken coop, chewing his *Brot* carefully and watching Roberto. The moment felt heavy and ready, like a late-fall apple. The slowness of everything suddenly filled Roberto with frustration and longing.

Roberto didn't even look around. He walked quickly past Enzo, straight into the chicken coop, as though he were invisible. Food, he said to himself, food was everyone's right. No one should starve. He had collected three eggs and was about to reach under the next hen for a fourth egg when he heard a scraping noise. He turned around.

Wasser stood in the doorway.

Roberto stopped still. He was caught. Finally. Everything seemed to stop. Every little noise, every little movement. The dust of the chicken coop made his eyes sting. It dried the inside of his nose. He sneezed.

Wasser didn't speak. He gestured with his chin for Roberto to come on out.

Roberto slowly looked at the eggs in his hands—the evidence of his crime. He turned to put the eggs in the closest nest, but the hen on that nest pecked at him and squawked. Stupid hen. Stupid Roberto. Dumb and slow and heavy and stupid. Both of them too hot in this coop—too hot to breathe.

Wasser pulled him by the arm backward out of the chicken coop, still holding the three eggs in both hands.

Roberto kept his eyes on those eggs. He stumbled along with Wasser pulling him. He put all his concentration into making sure the eggs didn't fall. If the eggs stayed whole, maybe nothing terrible would happen. He knew this was magic thinking. He knew it was crazy. But he had to keep those eggs whole. The butt of Wasser's gun stuck out of the holster. It was shiny and smooth. Like an eggshell.

Wasser walked him over to the driver of one of the trucks. They talked and pointed at the eggs and talked. Wasser laughed. Then he pushed Roberto ahead of him to the first truck, the only one completely unloaded. He gestured for Roberto to climb into the back.

Another journey. The thought exhausted him. Roberto looked at the three eggs, still intact. They couldn't help him. Nothing could help him now. He held out the eggs to Wasser. Wasser shook his head. Roberto placed the eggs gently on the ground. Wasser shouted at him. Roberto picked them up. If he put the raw eggs in his pockets and tried to climb into the truck, they'd probably break. He opened his mouth wide and put one egg inside each cheek and the third on his tongue. He climbed into the truck and sat with his back against the cab, looking at Wasser.

Wasser laughed again.

"Excuse me, sir."

Wasser turned around.

Enzo stood there. He stood tall, his shoulders squared. He was only a head shorter than Wasser, but he had half his girth. "I stole eggs, too." He gestured the act of reaching for an egg, then popping it in his mouth. "I did it, too." His voice grew louder and trembled slightly. "I'd rather die than let my friend take the punishment alone, you big lump of pig dung." His face was expressionless and he spoke in a monotone. He pulled the Saint Christopher medal out from inside his shirt and ran it back and forth along the chain. "As this saint, whatever his name is, is my witness, I stole eggs, and I'd like to puke them all over your fat head."

Roberto sat immobile in the truck. He was stunned. It made no sense for both of them to get in trouble. And he couldn't believe Enzo had called Wasser names. Enzo, of all people, could never afford to be reckless, even for a moment. All the remaining energy went out of Roberto's body, as though he would collapse. As though he were the woman hit by the rock, who wouldn't stand up again. This was it. Everything was over.

Wasser barked at Enzo to get into the truck. Then he walked off, while another soldier watched them both.

Roberto took the eggs out of his mouth and set them in his lap. "Why did you do that? Why did you tell him?"

"If you left, I'd slowly starve. Whatever happens to us now, it can't be worse than that."

It was true. Roberto put his hand over the lump in his pocket—the lump that was the stone the girl had given him. She would starve. Her little sister would starve. How could he have let himself get caught like that?

And now anger welled up—anger at himself and at Enzo. "Why did you call him names, on top of it? If he understood, everything would have been much worse."

"The other Italian boys can't even understand Venetian dialect when we speak fast, so how can he understand us?"

Roberto still shook his head. "He could have been pretending not to understand just so he could hear us say secrets."

"That's ridiculous. Anyway, what did I say that was so bad?"

"You said you wanted to puke on him."

"I did, didn't I?" Enzo's voice was full of wonder.

Roberto nodded.

"I do. I want to puke on him." Enzo took a deep breath. "It's a good thing it was Wasser and not Arbeiter. Arbeiter would have killed you, for sure. And me, too."

A shiver ran through Roberto. Arbeiter was probably suspicious of him after the incident with the stones today. He probably watched Roberto carefully whenever he happened to see him. Arbeiter was the one who was most likely to have caught Roberto in the chicken coop, but it was Wasser who did. Wasser.

"Wasser actually thinks he's nice to us. He's just a dumb jerk, but Arbeiter's a real sadist." Enzo shook his head. "We're still alive because of Wasser."

"Maybe not."

"Huh?"

"Maybe someone else saved us." Roberto touched the medal around Enzo's neck. "His name is Saint Christopher. He watches over travelers."

Enzo looked solemnly at Roberto. Then he took an egg and held it up high. "To Saint Christopher," he said.

Roberto raised an egg. "To Saint Christopher." They cracked them together, and raw egg ran down their arms.

Enzo licked his off. "Might as well not waste them. Who knows if we'll ever eat again."

Roberto licked his off, too. Raw egg was actually close to delicious mixed with the salty sweat on his arm.

Wasser came back. He looked at them and laughed. He

handed them each a wurst. He said something. He gestured for them to eat up.

Roberto took his wurst and looked quickly at Enzo.

Enzo took the wurst. Then he grabbed the third egg from Roberto's lap and dropped the wurst in its place. "I prefer eggs," he said to Wasser. "Eggs, you dumb goathead."

Roberto put the second wurst in his pocket. He ate the first wurst.

Enzo ate the third egg.

Wasser shook his head at Enzo, but he didn't say anything. And in that moment Roberto realized Enzo was right: Wasser felt benevolent toward the boys in his charge. He didn't see them as prisoners. He had no sense of their homesickness or hunger. The enormity of Wasser's stupidity left Roberto aghast.

The other soldier got into the front of the truck and revved up the engine. Wasser waved. He put both hands on his belly and said something and nodded. He waved again.

Enzo hooked his arm through Roberto's. He sat straight, his chin high. Roberto tried to do the same.

They could hear Wasser's laugh as they rolled down the road.

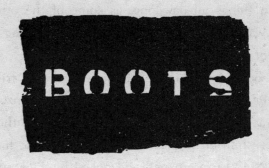

BOOTS

Roberto smoothed his blanket
flat. It wasn't really a blanket; it was an empty cement sack,
but in his head he called it his blanket. He wrapped it
around himself, tucking it up under his armpits. It covered
most of his abdomen that way. He tied it in place with a
rope, which he passed around his chest twice. His blanket
was his only possession besides the clothes on his body and
the hemisphere stone the Polish girl had given him—he
kept his blanket with him at all times. The air was cold.
Eastern Europe in late fall was colder than the coldest winter days in Venice, but Roberto resisted the temptation to
untie his blanket and wear it as a jacket. Without his blanket to crawl into at night, he would freeze to death. There
was no doubt about that. He couldn't risk wearing it out
by poking holes for his arms and head and letting it get

caught in things all day long, as some of the other boys did. Anyway, if he was lucky, they'd be working all day. Work kept him warm.

He shook Enzo's shoulder till he was sure his friend was awake. Roberto was an early riser by nature. Enzo wasn't. But it was important that Enzo get up before the others and relieve himself in privacy. So Roberto woke him without fail. Now Enzo groaned and poked his face out of his blanket. He opened his eyes and looked up at the sky; then he closed them again and rolled over on the hard ground. Roberto didn't worry; this was Enzo's routine.

Roberto let his eyes travel across the rows of sleeping boys. The nights of sleeping in the barn at the farm work camp seemed luxurious compared to bedding down on the open dirt here.

A wolf howled in the distance. Other wolves joined in. That was odd. Usually the howls started at twilight, when the temperature dropped to freezing or below, and continued intermittently till Roberto fell asleep. The sound didn't worry him, in any case. Wolves, even in a large pack, wouldn't approach a camp with so many people; Enzo had assured him of that. He said that it probably wasn't a big pack, anyway. Most of the wolves of Ukraine were in the forests of the Carpathian Mountains, not here in the great valleys.

It turned out that Enzo had read a lot about nature. He

was the one to spot the cyclone off in the distance a few weeks back. He said warmer weather would follow for a day or two afterward, and he was right. He was the one who named the long, low, slinky creatures they'd seen racing at the edge of the woods one dusk—weasels. He could even name some of the trees: hornbeam and oak and ash. Things a boy from Venice had never seen except in photographs.

Enzo wove these bits of their surroundings into the bedtime stories he still told every night. And he wove in their mothers and their fathers and Sergio and Memo and the canal near the big wooden bridge of the Accademia under the midnight moon and the winding staircase called the Bovolo that looked like a snail shell and oh so many things of Venice that made Roberto's heart want to keep pumping against all odds. All good things happened in Enzo's stories. Every child ate sweet grapes and walked in summer heat. Any threat was easily foiled. Those stories gave the only truly peaceful moments of Roberto's day.

Roberto took off the piece of material from his head and untied the knot and shook it out. Then he put it back in place, careful to cover both ears and his forehead, tying it behind at the nape of the neck. The material was wool, and it kept his head warm. A few weeks back, one of the soldiers had died after a fever. The other soldiers burned all his belongings in fear of disease. But a boy from Bolzano snatched the soldier's wool blanket before it caught fire. The boys divided it up equally. Almost all of them had fashioned hats from their pieces.

Several of the boys had died, too. Not all from fever, though. Some had coughed themselves to death—great, wet, racking coughs. And some who hadn't managed to find sacks for blankets had frozen.

Roberto put his hands in his armpits and made his way past the sleeping boys. One of the disadvantages of the way he tied his blanket around his abdomen was that he couldn't put his hands in his pockets. But that was okay, too, because when he put his hands in his pockets, he felt the Polish girl's stone. As long as he wasn't feeling the stone, he could go hours without thinking about her, without wondering what had become of her.

Sometimes he thought of throwing the stone away. He didn't know why he kept it.

The skin on his arms had already turned a white-blue, just from being exposed for those few minutes since he woke. This was the coldest day yet. But his legs were covered, at least. That's because Roberto had been the first to discover one of the frozen boys. And the first to discover a body got his choice of whatever clothing he wanted before the others pillaged it. The boy had a short-sleeved shirt, like Roberto. But he had trousers instead of shorts. So now Roberto wore trousers.

The trousers were short for him—his ankle and part of

his calf stuck out—but he loved them. He'd offered to share them with Enzo, trading pants every other day. Enzo seemed to suffer from the cold even more than Roberto did. But Enzo was so tall, the trousers weren't much of an improvement over shorts. So after the first time of trading, Enzo said the trade didn't make sense. And Roberto got to wear the trousers every day. He felt slightly guilty about it, but it wasn't his fault the boy who had died had been short.

And Enzo had better shoes than Roberto, anyway. His original shoes were still holding out pretty good. Roberto, on the other hand, had outgrown his shoes sometime that fall. He'd worn holes through the toes. It wouldn't have been much of a loss, given the holes he'd worn in the bottom as well, except for the bitter cold of the ground, even then. But Roberto had been lucky: Another boy discovered a body a few days later with boots. Not the high, thick boots that the German soldiers wore, but good boots, nonetheless. They came up over the ankles, and the laces were still in place. So that boy took the boots and left his own shoes—shoes big enough for Roberto's feet and with only one hole in the bottom of the left shoe. Roberto had moved swiftly to grab them. The hole hardly mattered, for Roberto and Enzo had ripped up a bloody shirt Enzo found in the back of a truck they were unloading and wrapped their feet inside their shoes. There was enough material to go around each foot twice.

Roberto stood at the edge of the sleepers now and hiked

up his blanket carefully. He relieved himself into the small
ditch they'd dug when they first made camp here—when
the ground was still workable. Enzo joined him, his blanket tied around his shoulders like a cape. Enzo's blanket
was a potato sack, so it was pliable enough to tie, but it
was no warmer than a cement sack. Their breath made
white balls of vapor in front of their faces. Their urine
streams made the frozen dirt hiss. Winter came early to
this part of Ukraine, wherever this part of Ukraine was.
The only thing Roberto knew for sure was that it was far
from any settlements. The whole idea was for the Germans
to have an airstrip here, near enemy lines, so they could
refuel planes on their way to and returning from attacks on
Russian airports, factories, and cities.

They had come all the way here in the backs of
trucks—one truck after another, across the whole of
Poland. Then they'd turned southeast down into Ukraine.
At times it was slow going. The rain came relentlessly, and
the roads turned to mud deeper than a hand, then deeper
than an arm. The dry days that followed were actually the
hardest because the mud solidified into ruts and high
ridges, so that even the big wheels of the trucks couldn't
roll over them. That's when the boys would get out of the
trucks and pick at the road until it was passable.

The boys were good at picking and digging and everything else, for only the strongest, best workers wound up

in Eastern Europe. Especially if they had caused trouble at their last work camp. Roberto had been told this. The Italian boys in this camp tried hard to understand one another. They brought out their school Italian and struggled along with that when necessary. But most of the time each spoke in his own dialect, slowly and carefully. Roberto found that if he just loosened his ear up a bit, he could understand most of what was being said to him, even though the boys who weren't from the Veneto region had a lot of trouble understanding Roberto. They said Venetian dialect was a totally different language. Still, Roberto noticed that when they truly needed to understand him, they did.

Language was prized among the boys; language was necessary for plotting. They were constantly plotting a theft of cigarettes or food. Now and then they plotted escape. There was still a sense of each boy for himself—but there was also a sense of strength in unity. And the German soldiers knew that. They watched the boys more attentively than in the old camp. But they never beat them. They wanted them strong and able to work. And it was something more, too; the soldiers were kinder here than in the last work camp. It was as though being isolated in the wilds of Ukraine had made all of them comrades somehow.

Roberto wasn't hungry anymore—or at least not in the same way. They ate worse than at the work camp in Poland—nothing but watery soup; a small piece of *Brot*, of course; and the garbage left by the soldiers. But he had grown accustomed to his lot and his stomach hardly ever growled, even though his mind sometimes still conjured up images of grilled sea bass and fluffy gnocchi. And when his stomach did growl sometimes at night, he took out a soupbone he had snatched from the garbage and sucked on it, even though it had long ago become dry as old leather.

Enzo carefully inspected anything that resembled meat before eating it. Roberto knew the things they ate were hardly recognizable as food, so the inspection was unreliable. Still, he nodded in agreement when Enzo declared the meat to be something other than pork.

None of the boys complained about the food with each other. But they plotted to steal the occasional fresh vegetables reserved for the soldiers, or a container of sour milk, or a sweet cake. And sometimes the theft plots ended in success. Roberto had never considered carrots anything special before—now they were a treasure.

He thought about the Polish girl back in the pen at the last work camp, and his yearning for more food suddenly seemed obscene.

Shame made his ears hot. At least that was a comfort. If only he could get away from here. Away and away and away, escape from the soldiers, from the knowledge that soldiers existed.

Once an escape plot among the boys had actually succeeded. Three boys had crawled under the tarp of an empty truck one night and been transported out of camp the next morning. They planned to jump off as soon as they found themselves on the outskirts of a town. They would follow train tracks and somehow get on a train going west. No one knew if they made it home. But everyone said they did. No one talked about the fact that they had to make it across Poland, which had fallen to the Germans at the very beginning of the war—so noplace, utterly noplace, in Poland was German-free—and then across Czechoslovakia and Austria, both under German rule.

Roberto didn't like to speculate on those boys. When he and Enzo had been driving here in the back of the truck with a handful of other Italian boys, they'd listened for train whistles. They'd paid attention to whatever the tires of their truck crossed over—especially to train tracks. They, too, had thought about jumping out and hitching a ride on a train. Venetian boys didn't really think in terms of kilometers; Roberto had always before measured distance in how many minutes it took to walk someplace. But the boys from cities on the mainland could estimate long distances well. They said the tracks crossed this land at intervals of fifty to one hundred kilometers. That was a lot. A person could walk all day through interminable black pine forests, only to wait for a train that might be going too fast to jump onto—or going in the wrong direction—or that had no open freight-car doors—or that was full of soldiers with guns.

Roberto tried to talk the three boys out of their escape plan. He listed all the obstacles. They acted like they didn't understand him; they brushed him off and whispered to each other in excited bursts. And a few days later they were gone.

The soldiers hadn't made a big deal of the escape. The tarmac was already completed by then, and the only real work left was to refuel the planes when they landed and keep the airstrip in good shape. It was work they could do easily. Roberto expected that the only reason some of them hadn't already been sent on to a new location to build another airstrip was that it was too late in the season to work the earth.

"The air hurts today," said Enzo. "My bones ache. I feel like an old man. Like my father." He leaned back on his heels and stretched in spite of the cold. "I wish he knew I was thinking of him."

Roberto rubbed his arms up and down; then he put his hands back in his armpits. He had to find cloth to wrap his hands soon. He didn't know how much longer he could go without getting frostbite. But as long as his fingers hurt, he was okay. He thought of his own father's aches and pains. Sometimes after a day of good business, his father would be so stiff from standing in the rear of the gondola all day that he couldn't sit. He'd stand in the kitchen and Roberto and Sergio would rub his legs and massage his back and neck until the knotted muscles finally yielded and he could bend his knees and rest in the chair that was reserved for him alone.

Had winter come to Venice yet? Roberto wasn't sure, but he thought it was around the middle of November. Probably there were high waters in Venice now. Probably his father had lots of extra jobs transporting people across flooded *campo*s.

Roberto thought suddenly of the Campo Santa Margherita and the wonderful ice cream store there. How could he be thinking of ice cream on such a cold morning? But there it was, creamy *gianduia*—chocolate with hazelnut flavoring. He opened his mouth instinctively. The cold air pierced his throat. He rubbed his throat, then his cheeks, then his eyes. "Oh, Enzo!" He pointed.

Roberto and Enzo walked around the ditch. A few meters back in the dirt lay two German soldiers. The boys walked closer. The soldiers were gray-faced and lifeless. A bottle lay shattered on the ground nearby. Roberto smelled it: really strong vodka—probably close to pure alcohol. One of the bodies still clutched another empty bottle. It was the same soldier who had let the Italian boys have a taste one night not long before. The soldier had done it secretly—not letting the other soldiers know. He was always the nicest to the Italian boys. Vodka was terrible stuff, though. Roberto had gagged when he tasted it.

Roberto knelt beside that soldier and fingered the sleeve of his uniform. The Germans were clothed well compared to the Italian boys, but their clothing was still too thin for this weather. They'd passed out and frozen to death. Roberto stared at this soldier's face. He wasn't really all that many years older than Sergio—maybe eighteen or nineteen, at the oldest—but he looked ageless now. Like a grandfather. Death made him ancient overnight.

"The poor idiots. We could take their clothes. Trousers. Gloves. Everything." Enzo spoke in a whisper. "We could get out of here."

Only what if a Soviet farmer saw them in German uniforms and shot at them before they could explain? And how would they explain? They were Italians, after all, and Italy was at war with these people. And how far would they have to walk to the nearest train? And the dead soldiers were bigger than Roberto and Enzo. Their clothes would hang limp on them. But Enzo was already tugging at the boots of the other soldier.

The boots were good. No matter what, those boots were worth having. Roberto pulled at the boots of his soldier.

"Look!" One of the Italian boys stood pointing from the far side of the ditch.

And now a group formed.

Roberto had the boots off and was pulling at the trousers. Enzo was still struggling with the second boot of his soldier.

A German soldier came up. He shouted in alarm. He leveled his rifle.

Enzo stood up fast, both hands raised with a boot in each one. "Stand up, Roberto. Raise your hands!"

Roberto gritted his teeth. It would take only another few minutes. The soldier's trousers were long—long enough for Enzo, and Enzo couldn't bear much more of this cold. Roberto yanked off the trousers and started on the shirt. He worked like a madman, his half-frozen fingers fighting the frost-covered buttons.

The soldier fired.

The bullet went over Roberto's head.

Enzo dropped the boots and pulled Roberto to his feet.

"No!" Roberto struggled to get free. "We can be warm. Warm, Enzo."

Enzo held him tighter. He raised Roberto's hands with his, over their heads. "Stay alive. Please, Roberto, stay alive."

Roberto blinked. His eyes darted all around. Then they came to rest on Enzo's face, on his steady black eyes. He breathed evenly again.

"That's good. Real good." Enzo loosened his grip and the two of them faced the soldier.

The soldier came around the ditch, his gun pointed at them. His face showed fear. The only two other soldiers in the camp came running. They held their rifles out in front, at the ready. They yelled as they came. The boys on the other side of the ditch backed off.

The first soldier looked across the scene. He kicked the vodka bottle from the dead soldier's hand. He said something over his shoulder to the other two soldiers. Then he picked up one pair of boots and handed them to Roberto. He handed the other pair to Enzo. He shouted and gestured for them to get back on the far side of the ditch.

Roberto ran with his boots clutched to his chest. The madness that had grabbed him when he was stripping the soldier was entirely gone now. It was too bad he couldn't have kept the trousers for Enzo. And, oh, if they could have had the long-sleeved shirts. And the gloves. But they both had boots now, and boots were wonderful. It was only the start of winter; the boots would serve them well. He sat down and put them on.

Enzo sat beside him, pulling on boots, too. "Two against three. That's the best odds we'll ever see again. We could have grabbed the guns. We could have shot them before they knew what was happening."

Roberto didn't answer. For the first time Enzo's fighting words irritated him. What was the point? They both knew very well why they hadn't grabbed the dead soldiers' guns. Even if they could have brought themselves to shoot the three other soldiers—and Roberto wasn't sure they could— it would have been no use. Where would they go from here? They'd starve before they got there. Or freeze. Or get shot. But one thing was certain: They'd die without the German soldiers to watch after them. They were trapped.

They'd been trapped since that afternoon in the movies in Mestre. Roberto thought of the boys who had snuck away in the back of the truck. The conviction that they were now dead lay heavy on Roberto's chest.

Why couldn't Enzo admit it? Why did he have to persist in those stupid, meaningless fighting words? Roberto shook his head. He stood up and walked off to breakfast.

The boys spent the day leveling the airstrip, filling in recent holes, clearing off broken branches and rocks that had been blown there by the night winds. They knew that they'd be allowed to sleep late and when they woke in the morning, a plane would land for refueling. That's how it always happened.

But it didn't work out that way.

Roberto woke in the still of night. Something was different. At first he didn't know where he was. Everything was cloudy white and noisy in the dim moonlight. It had snowed and it was still snowing, hard. And there was scuffling next to him. Enzo screamed. Roberto jumped to his feet. That's when he realized he was barefoot. They'd slit the bottom of his cement-sack blanket and stolen his boots. And someone had snatched up his old shoes as soon as he'd taken them off. Now he'd have to find something else to serve as shoes—maybe another ripped-up cement sack—otherwise, his feet would freeze. They'd be bloody, frozen stumps. If he didn't get something on his feet soon, he was as good as dead. Enzo screamed again. Enzo was fighting them. It was hard to see in the night, with the blanket as part of the fray. But Enzo was fighting for his boots—for his life.

Roberto shouted and jumped into the middle of it. He shouted and shouted at the top of his lungs. He swung his fists and beat whoever he could reach. He got knocked in the head, in the chest. He got thrown to the ground.

A shot went off in the night sky. A soldier yelled. The thieves disappeared into the dark.

Roberto got to his knees. "Enzo?" He crawled to the crumpled form.

"They didn't get my boots, Roberto." Enzo's voice was barely a whisper. "I tried to keep them from taking yours, but one was already off before I woke and realized what was going on. I'm sorry."

"It's all right, Enzo. I'll get my old shoes back from whoever took them."

"No, you won't. No, you'll wear these boots. When I die, they're yours."

"No." Roberto lifted Enzo's head and back onto his lap. "Don't die. Please don't die."

"I have to. That's what this war is about." Enzo held on to Roberto's shirt.

Roberto had to lean over to hear Enzo now.

"I'm going to freeze to death."

"No! I won't let you freeze." Roberto tucked his own blanket and Enzo's blanket around them both. Enzo's headcloth had come off in the fight. Roberto picked it up now and tied it on carefully. Then he lay down beside Enzo, cradling him in his arms. He breathed hot on Enzo's forehead. He couldn't see Enzo's bruises in the dark, but he had seen others recover from savage beatings. Others recovered. Others recovered.

"You'll have to tell yourself stories now," said Enzo in the softest whisper. "Do it. Do it to keep your spirit strong."

"I will."

"Don't forget. Please."

"I won't."

"And fight, Roberto. Even though you hate it. I know you hate it."

Roberto nodded. "I do, I hate it."

"So do I. But you have to fight. I don't mean with your fists. I mean inside. Don't ever let them win over the inside of you."

Roberto thought of how annoyed he'd been with Enzo's fighting words only yesterday morning. He was grateful he hadn't said anything about it to Enzo then. "I understand. I'll fight."

"Speak Venetian all the time. Remember who you are."

"I can't speak it without you."

"You have me." Enzo patted Roberto softly on the chest. "Here. You have me."

"Yes." Roberto's eyes filled with tears. "Yes, you're in my heart."

"You're a good friend, Roberto."

"So are you, Enzo. The best."

"I wish I could keep living, just to see this war through with you." He smiled. "How lucky I've been to have you for a friend."

Roberto could hardly talk. "Me, too."

The snow fell. Hour after hour. Roberto stayed awake, brushing it off the tips of Enzo's hair, which stuck out from the headcloth. He rubbed Enzo's back under the blanket. He kept him warm.

The snow still fell. When it stopped, the stars came out. They sparkled in patterns all over the heavens. Roberto didn't recognize any of the constellations. It was as though he was looking at the sky for the first time. The brightness of the stars promised a clear day ahead. He slept at last, until the first weak streaks of sun crossed the sky.

Roberto shook Enzo.

Enzo didn't respond.

Roberto rocked back and forth on the ground, holding Enzo's body tight, keeping it warm, though it no longer mattered. Sadness blanketed their world. Roberto curled over and whispered hoarsely in Enzo's ear, "You didn't freeze. At least you didn't freeze."

THE WOODS

Roberto stood in German boots, in the boots Enzo had bequeathed to him just hours ago. He watched the bomber land. The boys had spent the morning clearing snow off the runway. They scurried around in practiced harmony. Everyone knew their duties without being told. Everything was getting done without Roberto's help. Everything from now on till forever would get done without Enzo's help.

Roberto hadn't even been able to bury Enzo's body. The ground was too hard to dig anymore—it was even too hard to pick. He had let the other boys take Enzo's clothes, except his underwear. He'd screamed when someone tried to take Enzo's underwear. He'd pummeled the boy with both fists. Roberto, who never raised a hand against anyone, had thrown himself into the scuffle last night and acted like a raging bull this morning. Then he'd insisted on wrapping Enzo in his blanket. He knew the living boys needed the blanket and Enzo didn't. Everyone knew that. They looked at him as though he were crazy. But he wouldn't leave Enzo white in the snow like that. And he couldn't bear to look at Enzo's crushed chest. The boys must have broken half his ribs last night.

One of them walked around now in German boots—the boots he'd stolen off of Roberto in the night. Roberto stared at the boy. The boy didn't lower his head. He didn't look ashamed.

The boys would steal Enzo's blanket as soon as Roberto left his side. They would steal it without shame.

They would steal his underwear, too.

Then they'd know.

He wasn't Enzo anymore—he was Samuele again. In death he could carry his true name.

Would it matter to the boys?

It would matter to the German soldiers.

And everyone knew Roberto and Samuele were like brothers. They had given up trying to hide their friendship when they'd come to the Ukraine work camp.

Roberto was doomed.

Two Germans got out of the bomber and consulted with the three German soldiers left in the work camp. The Italian boys immediately set to work on the bombs. No one looked at Roberto, standing with his legs in a straddle. No one had looked at him all morning. It was as though they had all agreed, both boys and soldiers, that Samuele's death had turned Roberto temporarily insane and it was best to leave him alone. For now. It wouldn't last, though. They'd get angry if he acted crazy too long.

A promise is to keep. Roberto would die fighting inside, as he had promised Samuele.

He walked over to the supply pile and grabbed a shovel. The snow was soft and fluffy, easy enough to dig with his hands. But his fingers would freeze. So he made a trench in the snow with the shovel and pulled Samuele into it. He took off the blanket. The Saint Christopher medal was frozen to Samuele's broken chest. Roberto winced. Samuele hadn't said one word about how much it hurt.

Samuele needed something more. He deserved something more. Roberto had been to only one funeral in his life—his grandfather's. He was five at the time, and all he remembered now was that there were lots of words. That's what Roberto could give Samuele—parting words, in Venetian dialect, just as Samuele would have wanted them.

"Goodbye, Samuele. I'll miss you." He swallowed to keep the tears from falling. "I miss you already." Roberto didn't look around. He wouldn't know who witnessed him tending to the body of his Jewish friend—he wouldn't care. No one could conquer the inside of him. He bent and put one hand on Samuele's heart and the other on his own heart. "You're my best friend. Rest now."

Roberto straightened. He swallowed over and over. Finally he grabbed the shovel and piled snow over Samuele until he was completely covered. He rolled the potato-sack blanket into a ball and walked back to the supply pile and dropped the shovel. Then he kept walking, through the stand of trees beside the camp.

He hadn't known what he was going to do until he found himself doing it. It was like the time he walked to the fence when the Polish Jews were first put in the pen at the farm work camp. He hadn't even realized he'd stood up. And it was like the final time he went into the chicken coop—when he just did it without looking around first. Other forces pushed rational thought aside and moved his body forward without reason.

Roberto thought of pushing the material on his head up to expose his ears so that he could hear shouts from behind and prepare himself for the bullets. But he didn't. It would be less scary to just get shot and drop dead.

He walked slowly at first, but he didn't trudge. An energy pulsed through him, an energy born out of knowing that, quite simply, he had nothing to lose. In that knowledge lay a delicate but undeniable triumph.

He walked, head high. And the triumph turned to exhilaration.

He walked.

Then, when the bullets didn't come, and when he finally realized they weren't coming, he went faster. He ran. And now he was deep, deep into the trees and he couldn't hear the noises of the camp any longer. He stumbled to a stop. His heart pounded and he couldn't catch his breath. He looked around. He was alone; no one had followed.

He shook out Samuele's blanket and threw it across his shoulders, covering his bare arms at last. His blood raced with the surprising knowledge that he had a chance at escape. How stupid he'd been not to have given escape any true forethought. He could have tried to take something along—the shovel, at least. But it never crossed his mind that he would actually get beyond their view alive. He hugged himself in the blanket. He'd brought Samuele's blanket just to have a part of Samuele with him when he died. Now it would be his best chance at survival.

He knew directions from the rise of the sun, so he headed due south. Italy was far to the south and to the west, as well. The shortest path would have been southwest. But his thought now was to get someplace warmer as fast as possible. And due south was warmer.

His mind made the calculations. From all these months of manual labor, he'd grown strong. He was used to working ten to twelve hours a day. And he had a good sense now of how far a kilometer was. If he walked for as many hours as he worked every day, without slowing down, he could cover a good seventy to eighty kilometers in a single day, at the least. How far could he be from the Black Sea? Three days? A week? Not more. For sure, not more.

The trees finally ended at a huge open expanse. The sun got stronger. Last night's snow melted away. Walking became a slippery affair. Roberto had to slow his pace. But he never stopped. And he never looked back.

Midmorning he worked his hand into his pocket under the cement-sack blanket tied around his abdomen and took out the *Brot* from breakfast. He'd almost given it to the boy next to him because he felt like he never wanted to eat again. Thank heavens he hadn't. His hunger ravaged him now. But he kept control: He put half back in his pocket; then he ate the other half in small nibbles, making it last as long as possible.

At lunchtime he ate the rest of the *Brot*—no, the bread. He wasn't with the Germans anymore; he would use Venetian words for everything.

At dusk he took out his old soupbone and gnawed on it.

He never stopped walking. But dark came earlier these days, and he had to find a place to spend the night soon. He resented the night. He needed to get to the Black Sea fast. Then he would follow the coastline westward to Turkey and through the strait to the Mediterranean. Once he got to the Mediterranean, he knew he could make it home.

How far was it to Venice?

So far. Oh, so far.

But that was the wrong way to think about it. He had to keep control, to set his sights on one goal at a time. The Black Sea. He could reach the Black Sea. That was manageable.

He scanned the horizon. A little to the east he saw a line of trees. He didn't want to go east. He would veer to the west if he had to, but going east only took him away from everything he needed.

Still, he needed to get out of the open before night. The unbroken wind at night could freeze him, even with two blankets.

He went east. He forced himself to go fast. He didn't run; he wouldn't risk falling. The ground was soggy from melted snow, and he couldn't risk getting his clothes wet. He swung his legs in large, even strides in those big German boots.

It was pitch black by the time he reached the first tree. A spruce. The whole stand was spruces. He had seen spruces far to the north when he'd traveled to this work camp in the back of the truck. But once they'd headed south, the trees had turned to oaks and pines. Now here suddenly was a stand of spruce. Bad luck. It was impossible to climb a spruce. He'd have to sleep on the ground. Without the protection of the other boys.

And now the awful thought came to him: Alone he was perfect wolf meat.

He stood stupidly in the dark, not knowing what to do. An owl hooted. There was no wind here among the trees. And the air was different—heavier, wetter. He was suddenly exhausted.

Something moved quickly through the trees to his right. Low to the ground. Roberto's heart leaped.

Whatever it was, it passed. It didn't notice him.

Why not?

Because there was no wind to carry his scent. Samuele had taught him how important scent was to predators like wolves. Only if they crossed the path he had traveled would they smell him. Roberto had to find a way to break the scent trail.

He relieved himself against a tree. The smell of his urine was strong. Passing wolves couldn't miss it. They'd come to this tree. Even if he could climb it, they'd know he was there. They'd circle the bottom and trap him.

Roberto looked around. He couldn't stand there forever. Noises came from the tops of the trees. The night creatures were moving into action. The cold on his cheeks grew perceptibly stronger. The scent of spruce overwhelmed.

That was it: the spruce scent. If he could mask his path with spruce scent, nothing would find him.

Roberto broke off two densely needled bottom branches. He held the thick end in each hand, with the needles flopping on the ground. He slapped a branch down in front of him, still holding fast to one end. He stepped on the branch. He slapped the other branch down in front of him and stepped on it. He traveled that way along the edge of the spruce thicket for a long time. If he was lucky, the wolves would think they'd treed him back where he'd relieved himself. If he was lucky, the spruce branches under his feet would hide the scent of his boots.

Some of the spruces at the very edge of the thicket had boughs that reached to the ground. He crawled under one, to the small pocket of space close to the trunk. The branches scratched at the back of his head. Not a perfect lair. Still, the ground was surprisingly dry. He made a bed of the broken branches he had carried there. Then he untied his own blanket from around his chest and rolled himself up in both blankets, covering even his head. Within minutes he felt snug. The thick branches above offered good protection if it snowed again, the broken branches below offered a cushion against the hard ground, and the blankets did the rest. He wouldn't freeze tonight.

He told himself a Bible story Samuele had told him, of the three Jews that King Nebuchadnezzar sent into the furnace. He described out loud the flames that licked at the three men and at the angel who joined them. He felt their victory when they emerged from the furnace unsinged. It was the hottest story he could remember. It warmed him to his ears. Then he fell asleep.

Roberto woke in the dark. He pushed up on his elbows with a start. His head hit a branch; his stomach growled. Was it just hunger that woke him or something else? He listened. He heard birdcalls from what seemed far away. He crawled out from under the branches. It was late morning already, but the branches were so thick, they'd kept out the sunlight. He tied his blanket to his abdomen, like always, and wrapped Samuele's blanket around his shoulders and arms.

He walked through the trees searching for pines. Pine nuts wouldn't make a bad breakfast. But all were spruces. He picked up a spruce cone and split open the back of a section. The cone was dry. He couldn't even tell if there had ever been a nut there—the whole thing crumpled away in his hand.

He heard something welcome, though: water. Nothing soothed Roberto faster than the presence of water. He followed the sound through the trees and came out on a stream. The placement of the trees and the slope of the land told him that in spring the stream ran wide. But now it was shallow and narrow and icy.

Roberto walked along the bank, looking carefully at the larger rocks that stuck out of the water. Finally he found one that was flattish on top, with a little pool in an indentation near its center. There was a smaller rock between the bank and that rock, so he leaped from the smaller one to the other. Then he stooped on the flattish rock and drank the water from the pool. It was cold, still—but the sun had done its job on the shallow pool and warmed it enough so that it didn't hurt his throat as it went down.

He jumped back to the bank. Even though his stomach had clearly shrunk since he'd been in Ukraine, hunger squeezed his insides. It hurt worse now than even at the farm work camp.

He searched for rocks about the size of his hand, half embedded in the mud at the edge of the stream. If there's one thing a Venetian boy knew, it was that water held food. He stuck his hands in the frigid water and turned over rocks, and more often than not, little things scurried off or dug themselves quickly into the mud. He had to be fast to catch any. On the next rock he was ready. He snatched instantly. Pinched between his thumb and index finger several pairs of little legs wiggled at him, sticking out from an almost translucent body in a thin, soft shell. His nostrils flared in disgust at the idea of eating it alive. He closed his eyes. He'd eaten raw clams before—lots of times. And raw sea urchins. They were probably still alive when he put them in his mouth. He opened his eyes and looked again at the flailing legs. It was the legs that made eating the creature alive seem awful—just the stupid little legs. "You can't be worse than a raw chick," he said aloud. He held his hand toward the heavens. "To you, Enzo." He ate. It wasn't so bad. The thought was worse than the act. So the trick was not to think.

He jammed his fingers down into the half-frozen mud and came up with a clump. He washed it in the water. It was some sort of shell-less snail. A slug. It was too big to eat all at once. Roberto took a deep breath. No thinking, he said to himself. He chomped the slug in half and swallowed. He waited a minute. He was okay. He looked down at his hand. The half of the slug that remained wiggled.

Roberto vomited.

He rinsed his mouth out with the cold, cold water. He couldn't act this way. Not if he wanted to live. He couldn't afford to be squeamish. He went to the next rock and lifted it and grabbed. Then he ate without even looking at what he caught. It didn't matter. After that, he ate blindly. Some of the creatures crunched in his teeth. Some slithered down his throat. It didn't matter. It was food.

He spent maybe half an hour on breakfast. Then he decided he had to move on. His hunger wasn't satisfied, but it would probably take constant eating all day to get satisfied on these tiny water creatures.

The stream ran southeast. Roberto wanted to go due south. But if he left the water, he might leave trees for a long time again. And how could he sleep without the protection of trees? How could he eat without the guarantee of water creatures?

He followed the stream all day, stopping only twice to eat. The woods thinned and thickened and thinned again.

When night came, he climbed a tree. He wedged himself between a wide branch and the main trunk. He felt fairly secure until he looked down: It was a long way down. He hugged the trunk, but the dizziness wouldn't go away. He took off the rope around the blanket on his abdomen. He arranged both blankets so that they covered his middle and arms and formed a hood he could retreat his whole head into. He secured them by making tucks at strategic points. Then he passed the rope behind his back and around the trunk of the tree and knotted it. There. Now he couldn't fall.

He had done everything he could to keep himself safe. He had moved almost mechanically, without hesitation. But now he sat silent in the tree and looked around. Roberto was alone. In the woods. In late fall. Far from anything familiar.

If only Samuele were with him. But he had done it the night before—he could do it again. He could bring Samuele by his side with the help of stories. He could raise

Samuele from his own heart. What story would Samuele tell tonight, out here? Roberto knew. He spoke aloud again. He described Moses going up onto Mount Sinai. Sitting in a cover of clouds, alone and hungry and without direction, for six long days. Then the Lord came in all His glory and gave Moses so many directions—how to build the tabernacle, what the priests should wear, how to keep the Sabbath.

Roberto was no Jew. But the Lord of those stories was his Lord, too. It would become apparent what Roberto should do next. He let his neck curl till his chin rested on his chest. He slept.

Oohoo!

Roberto woke to the call. Two beats, the first one louder. He had been dreaming of one of Samuele's own stories about a child high in a prison, looking down at the ground he couldn't reach. And now it was Roberto looking down. The ground shone white in the soft, waning moonlight. It had snowed.

He looked all around. The call that woke him had to have been an owl, a mere owl. But it was a different call from the owl's the night before. It was much louder. And very close.

Oohoo!

Roberto searched the trees with his eyes. He couldn't

spy the bird or any other animal. He knew the woods had
to be teeming with life, but everything knew how to blend
in or take cover. Something dangerous could be lurking behind any tree. He looked again. Nothing.

Dawn crept through the woods. If he climbed down
now and got an early start, he could make up for the fact
that he'd be slowed down by the snow. The owl had done
him a favor. He untied the knot in the rope and stuffed it
between himself and the trunk as he stretched his arms
and shoulders and neck. Then he tied Samuele's blanket
around his neck and wrapped the rope around his waist
three times. He tossed his own blanket free of the branches
and climbed down after it. He'd tie it around his abdomen
later, but first things first. He broke a low branch off the
tree to use for digging a latrine.

The snow was only a hand's depth, soft and powdery.
Roberto jammed the branch down hard on the frozen earth.
To his amazement, the ground yielded easily. It was all dead
leaves and twigs. He dug deeper. And now he could see—
this was the opening of an underground animal's burrow.

What kind of animal burrowed underground? Anything
dangerous? Venice had very few open places with dirt, and
what dirt there was held no burrows. But Roberto knew
about rabbit warrens. Did rabbits store food underground?
Maybe if he kept digging, he would find nuts or roots or
something else edible. He dug more vigorously.

A brown head popped up out of the snow a meter away. Then the whole furry little creature appeared and ran across the whiteness. There was a back door to the burrow. Another creature followed. Hamsters.

Hoo!

The raucous scream terrified him. Roberto jumped around and saw huge flapping wings, a great hooked beak, two round yellow eyes with tufts over them like devil's horns. He stumbled backward in surprise and fell. The owl grabbed a hamster in its talons and flew off. It was enormous. The wingspan was more than a grown man's height. It was brown and black, but its wings were flecked with white. And it disappeared in the treetops. Here and gone, in an instant.

Roberto hadn't known owls could come that large. He stood and brushed the snow off Samuele's blanket and muttered little words of gratitude that owls didn't eat people.

Then he laughed. An owl. An owl and funny, fat little hamsters, like in a pet store. He laughed out loud.

The yowl behind him made the hairs on his neck stand on end. He turned and faced the stare of the wolf. It stood but three meters away, its head held to one side at a steep angle. Its eyes glistened; the centers were deep black holes.

Roberto froze. He would never make it to a tree before the wolf got him. There was nothing to do but fight. The stick he'd been using for digging the latrine lay near his feet. He stooped and grabbed it quickly.

The wolf took a few steps forward. It staggered and stopped close to his blanket, which lay at the foot of the tree Roberto had slept in.

Roberto breathed hard through his mouth. He held the stick with both hands, ready to swing. In that moment he thought about what a pathetic gesture it was—to hold the stick like that—as though it mattered. Wolves ran in packs. Behind this one, others were coming. He couldn't see them; still, he knew they must be there.

But what else could he do? He gripped the stick with all his strength. And he remembered something Samuele had said. Wolves are loath to attack a full-sized, standing man. He would be fourteen in the spring—and he was average size for his age. He stood tall now. Look at me, wolf, he shouted inside his head—see how tall I am.

The wolf made an odd sound in its throat, almost as though it had a bone stuck there. Then its lower jaw dropped open. Its head leaned more and more to the side.

Slowly Roberto realized there was something wrong with the animal. Very wrong. It was sick. He took his eyes off the wolf just for a moment, to look beyond it through the trees. Nothing stirred. No eyes glowed. It might be a lone wolf, after all.

The wolf tucked its head back to the left and bit at its

rear paw. It wobbled. Twisted like that, all its ribs showed. It was emaciated.

This wolf was practically dead. Roberto could probably outrun it. But he needed his blanket first. He would never survive the cold without that blanket. It was essential.

Just a few steps—that's all it would take—and then he could bend down and reach out slowly and grab the edge of the blanket and run for dear life. The wolf might not even see him reaching, it was so busy chewing at its foot.

Roberto slowly took a step forward. Then another.

The wolf straightened its head and looked at him docilely. It seemed no more threatening than a house dog.

Roberto stepped forward again.

The wolf lunged in an instant transformation—fangs bared, eyes insane.

Roberto had only a second to raise the stick in defense.

The wolf snapped its jaws on the wood with a cracking sound. It wrenched the stick from Roberto and turned in a circle, then stopped, swayed, and fell on the blanket. Its eyes closed; white foam bubbled from its mouth.

Roberto turned and ran. He ran along the stream edge, stumbling over rocks, through scrubby bushes. He ran as fast as he could.

COLD

Roberto drank from the snow- fed water in the stream and shivered. He had left the wolf behind more than an hour ago, but the image of its maddened face lingered and kept him from thinking straight. He had to shake it off. He couldn't afford not to think straight.

He wore Samuele's blanket—now his only blanket—draped across his back and around his arms. He used the rope as a belt. It had been terrible luck that the wolf had fallen right on his blanket. No. No, it wasn't a matter of luck. It was Roberto's stupidity. He should have tied the blanket around his abdomen when he first climbed down the tree. He should have taken good care of it all the time—if he had, he'd still have two blankets.

Roberto straightened the blanket and took stock of his

situation. The stream promised a steady, if poor, food supply. The problem was that it headed southeast. Warmth was due south—and with only one blanket, he needed to get to a warm place fast. Winter was upon him; last night's snow was the start of the inevitable. It would get worse. Much worse. Everyone knew about Eastern European winters. He left the stream and walked south.

Roberto hoped the sun would warm up the land at least a little as the day went on. But it didn't. The wind was bitter behind him, and the snow stayed.

The land was much more sloping now, and stands of trees were rare. Roberto climbed from one hill to the next, always on the lookout for anything that moved. He saw a lone white rabbit, but he had no way to kill it. He thought of the hamster burrow back in the woods. It was a pity he hadn't gotten the chance to raid it for nuts. His lips were cracked and his teeth felt fuzzy and he was hungry, always hungry. He saw the tracks of deer. He ate snow in little bits to quench his thirst. He walked and as he walked, he talked to himself. After a while, his stomach actually hurt less somehow.

Then he saw them. They came over the crest of a hill. Tanks. Jeeps. Troops of soldiers. Mules. From this distance he couldn't tell whether they were Soviets or Germans. He stared for a moment, unbelieving. This was only his third day of being alone, but he'd come to think of the world as empty of humans. Of course it wasn't. The war was going on. People were killing each other.

Those soldiers might kill him.

He looked around for a place to hide. But he was already well past the last stand of trees, and if he tried to run back to them, he was almost sure to be seen. There was no vegetation whatsoever between him and the soldiers. Nothing to hide behind. Nothing to hide under. Except snow.

Snow.

He took the blanket off his shoulders and spread it on the ground. He covered it with snow. Then he snaked himself under it and peeked out the other side. He crawled along like that, on his belly, in the snow, covered by the camouflaged blanket. Snow caught at the collar of his shirt, then got shoved down inside, freezing him from his Adam's apple all the way down his sternum. He wrapped his hands and forearms in the corners of the covering blanket, but the snow scraped and burned at his upper arms. It hurt like fire. When he was close enough to see the soldiers well, he stopped.

They were a mixed group. The ones at the front, with the tanks, wore the German uniforms. The ones at the rear, with the mules, wore the Italian uniforms. The German soldiers had heavier boots, better coats. They walked in neat rows, with energy and assurance. The Italian soldiers were scraggly in comparison. They walked in scattered groups. Their shoulders slumped. They looked disheartened, even from where Roberto lay.

One soldier nudged another in the shoulder. They were talking. Maybe telling stories. Like Roberto and Samuele used to do. Roberto couldn't hear anything from this distance. He wished he could listen to their voices. He'd give a lot to hear Italian. He'd give a lot to hear a story and tell a story and not be alone, so alone.

But they all carried weapons, Germans and Italians alike. So it didn't matter if they held their heads high or not. And it didn't matter what language they spoke. They were all there for the same reason.

If Roberto showed himself, they'd surely feed him. And maybe they'd give him better clothes. But he'd be punished for running away from the work camp. And he'd definitely have to work for them somehow—he'd have to be part of this war again.

Roberto pressed both fists against his stomach to loosen the hunger knot, just as he had done so often when he was back at the farm work camp. He filled his mouth with snow to keep himself from shouting. He watched the soldiers go by. Keeping silent was hard—harder than facing the wolf.

He waited till they were out of sight. Then he stood up and shook the snow off the blanket. He was shivering uncontrollably by now. Lying on the snow had taken its toll.

And filling his mouth like that had been foolish. He needed to warm up. And fast. He rubbed the blanket hard on his arms and neck. He stamped his feet and walked in a circle and rubbed and rubbed. Then he wrapped himself as tightly as he could in the blanket.

He followed the trail of the soldiers, going where they'd come from. Somewhere along that trail there had to be station points for supplies. Somewhere there had to be food. Somewhere there had to be warmth.

He walked all afternoon.

He came to nothing. But the trail went generally south, so at least he was heading toward a warmer climate.

Night came. There were no trees to burrow under or climb up into. The moon was bright on the snow, so bright Roberto could still follow the soldiers' trail. He kept walking. Whether sleeping or moving, he was a target for whatever might be on the prowl—animal or human. Soldiers.

But he wasn't so sure anymore that he didn't want to be found by soldiers. It was cold. And it was growing colder as the night deepened. Freezing to death seemed more likely and more awful with every step.

Sometime in the middle of the night he saw the thing looming in the distance. At first it looked like a prehistoric monster from a nightmare. Part jutted up into the sky—a broken claw, scrabbling futilely at the stars. Pieces stabbed out in all directions. Roberto stood still and looked at it until he was sure it wasn't alive. Nevertheless, his jaw clenched and his ears buzzed with fear. He walked closer, and the smell of dead fire invaded his nose. A sick feeling grew in his stomach. There was something dreadfully wrong here.

He stood in front of what must have been a giant shed. It had been burned to the ground. And recently. No snow had fallen over the destruction yet. The thing in front of him was a mess of twisted metal. Some kind of contraption for farming—a reaper, maybe. And behind it was a burned-out tractor with a crank in front. The huge iron rear wheels had wide, flat spikes. It had been built to be indestructible in the field. But no one had thought of fire. Other unrecognizable things lay in the rubble.

The fire must have been tremendous—gigantic flames licking their way up toward the clouds. It must have been so hot. Oh, heavenly hot. If only he could have been nearby when it happened. If only he could have warmed himself in its glow.

Roberto looked around at the surrounding land. It was level here. And something about it made him know this had been fertile soil—a wonderful farm. He imagined it in warm days, thick with yellow wheat. He thought of the people baking heavy loaves of bread from that grain, sitting around tables, swapping stories as they ate.

He looked back at the charred remains. The people who

had worked this reaper, this tractor—they would have no way to prepare the earth this spring, no way to harvest it. They'd go hungry.

Roberto was hungry. And he was enormously sad. It was better that he hadn't been here to feel the fire. It hadn't been a heavenly heat—it had been hellish. It had been full of death.

He turned back to the soldiers' tracks, moving listlessly now. He wasn't sure he could stand to see what else lay along this trail.

If anything else lay along this trail.

Maybe he'd trudge forever. Endlessly.

He moved more and more slowly. The small clouds of his breath were spaced farther apart. Everything about him was slowing down. He stared with dry, stinging eyes into the nothingness. He tripped and fell. The snow rasped against his cheek, almost like wet sand. He got up with difficulty and looked around. Nothing. So much nothing. He would freeze here on this godforsaken trail in Ukraine. Roberto's tears left streaks that froze tight on his cheeks. He ran then, stumbling and crazy. He ran.

He was practically within calling distance of the small settlement before he realized it was houses and not just a clustering of bushes. He was so tired by now, he was becoming stupider by the minute. There was even a sign, undoubtedly and proudly saying the name of this village, though it was written in the Cyrillic alphabet and Roberto couldn't read a single letter of it. Blessed sign. Blessed village. A cat ran across the front of a house and disappeared around the corner.

Roberto walked along what was clearly the road through the village. He couldn't wait to see a human face, and at the same time he was terrified. Freezing was not the only way to die.

His boots crunched on the snow. It sounded shockingly loud to his ears. He expected someone to bolt from a house and shoot him dead before he could surrender. He lifted his hands to the moon. They shook with the cold. He coughed and his chest rattled, resounding in his head as though it were a hollow wooden ball holding a few dried beans. He turned in a circle, to give a full view. Anyone who took a moment to look him over, anyone who didn't just shoot at first sight, would know he was harmless. They had to know.

The houses were small, single-storied, and square. They had steepish roofs, rounded on the top. He counted eleven of them. There was no light anywhere, no spiral of smoke from a chimney, no sign of movement beyond that single cat.

The houses hadn't been burned. But something had happened here. Something bad.

He couldn't just stand there all night. In fact, the wind

was picking up in a fierce way. He probably couldn't stay standing more than a few more minutes. Even if there were no live hearths, these houses provided shelter from the sharp wind, and he needed to get to the other side of those doors now or never. He kept his hands high over his head, though they felt heavy as lead. He went up to the closest house. The front door stood partly open.

Somewhere in his head was the knowledge that he should have been alarmed at that fact. But he couldn't face that alarm right now. He needed shelter from the wind. He shivered violently. He put his face into the opening and called out, "Hello." But his voice came as a tiny croak.

No one answered. Nothing stirred.

He opened the door and stared into the blackness. "Hello. Is anyone here?" The room was cold and still. He couldn't make out anything at all in this dark—not the outline of furniture, nothing. It could have been totally empty, for all he knew. There was no warmth here. But at least there was no wind. He pulled the door shut behind him, dropped to the floor, and slept.

When Roberto opened his eyes, the boy sitting in the chair beside him jumped to his feet and held an ax high over his head. *"Lezhy!"* he shouted.

Roberto immediately lifted both hands.

The boy stamped his feet and jabbered something long and incomprehensible.

Roberto stared at the ax. The head was heavy enough to split his chest in one blow. He didn't move.

The boy spoke again. His eyes flicked around the room as he talked, then settled back on Roberto.

Roberto dared to look past him. The hearth was cold. A large black pot hung there, like in Roberto's kitchen at home. In Venice when frost came, his family slept in the kitchen in front of the fireplace, all of them together. It was toasty. This room should have been toasty now. Instead, Roberto could see his breath, almost as though he were still outside.

A table stood near the hearth with two chairs. There was a wide bed against one wall with a chest of drawers beside it. And on the floor in front of the chest was the body of an old man. He'd been shot in the neck.

Roberto's face went slack. He knew it. He knew it last night when he'd found the front door partly open. He'd known it even earlier, when he'd seen no smoke from the chimneys. He knew what had happened to this village.

Roberto looked back at the boy. "Was he your grandfather?"

The boy shook the ax and shouted fiercely, *"Stiy! Ne rukhaisia!"*

Roberto lifted his hands higher. The boy gripped the ax so tightly that the skin across his knuckles shone. His voice was strong and rough. But Roberto looked into his eyes now, and the boy's eyes gave him away. Roberto recognized that look—sheer desperation.

A desperate person could do unpredictable things— Roberto knew that. He'd left the last work camp out of desperation, and not even he could have predicted he'd do it.

But a desperate person welcomed company, too— Roberto knew that just as well.

He stood up slowly, keeping his eyes on the boy's face, trying to make his own face radiate comfort. He let his blanket fall to the floor. He rubbed his bare arms. He was taller than this boy—and older. The boy couldn't have been more than seven or eight. "I'm hungry," said Roberto softly. He rubbed his stomach. "I'm so hungry. Is there any food?"

The boy held the ax with both hands. He swung it hard, just to show he was ready to use it.

Roberto resisted the urge to step backward, away from the ax. "I'm not the enemy." He stood his ground and spoke in a level voice, a little louder now. "I'm hungry. And I bet you are, too." He walked over to the hearth, checking on the boy over his shoulder. But the boy just stood at the ready, watching. The shelves near the hearth had been ransacked. The soldiers must have raided anything they could find. Roberto moved beyond, to the chest, stepping carefully around the old man's body. He opened drawers till he found what he was looking for: a sweater. He pulled it on. Then he picked up his blanket and used it like a cape. He went out the door.

The boy came after him, always shouting rough words, always holding that ax.

Roberto went directly to the next house. The door had been bashed down. He wasn't surprised. He wasn't even horrified. The evil around him was numbing in a way. He stepped over the body of a woman and a girl without hesitation. That was the only way to get to the food shelves. And, yes, here was a burlap bag of buckwheat.

He turned to the boy, who was standing in the doorway watching him. "Where do we get water?"

The boy stared at him.

"*Wasser?*"

The boy just stared.

"All right, that's how it is. We'll just each talk and not have any idea what the other says. I'm used to that." Roberto picked up a pot and went out the door. The boy stepped aside as he passed, his eyes confused and tired. Roberto filled the pot with snow. He went back in and searched around the hearth till he found matches.

There was plenty of kindling in the corner. He threw two handfuls of it into the fireplace and struck a match. It went out without lighting anything. He struck another. The same thing happened. He felt the kindling carefully now. It was damp. He walked around the room touching surfaces. Everything was damp. Frost had formed overnight, then melted when the morning sun came in the windows. He knew because the chair in the corner was still covered with the cold sheen.

He needed something dry that would light easily. He needed paper. He looked around the shelves. There wasn't a single newspaper, magazine, book. Then he remembered the chest of drawers in the first house, where he'd found the sweater. There was no chest in this room, but there was a large trunk at the foot of the bed. He opened it. Yes, it was lined with brown paper, just as the chest in the other house had been. He emptied the trunk and ripped the paper from the sides and bottom. He crumpled it into a loose ball and put it in the fireplace. He struck a match.

Flames licked through the paper instantly. Roberto arranged the damp kindling around the edges, so it would dry. Then he fed the kindling to the fire, one piece at a time. Once the kindling burned, he went outside. Sure enough, there was a woodpile on one side of the house. He brushed the snow off the top of the pile and carried in two logs. He knelt and set them in the fireplace.

The weak fire touched the wet logs and hissed and spit and went out.

Roberto slumped back on his heels. He looked over his shoulder; the boy was gone. Roberto was all alone. If only Samuele were here. Or Sergio. Or Memo. Or anyone. The tears were hot on his cheeks.

He had to start all over again. He had to start all over again when he felt he could barely move.

But it would be all right. He just had to think, to act sensibly. He should have saved some of the paper from the trunk lining just in case. That wasn't sensible. He'd be more careful from now on. He sat up tall.

Where else could he find paper? He got to his feet and searched through every container in the house. Finally he found a tin full of loose tea leaves, lined with coarse paper. The leaves might burn, as well. He brought the tin over to the fireplace. Then he brought over the rest of the kindling. He'd built fires before, with his cousins at Easter time. They'd made bonfires outside and sat around talking late into the night. He shut his eyes and let himself remember the way they'd arranged the wood before they set it afire.

Roberto opened his eyes and went to work. He arranged the two logs in a V-shape. He made little pyramids of kindling in the middle. He saved the smallest pieces, the tinder, and shoved that into the center of each of the pyramids.

The boy stomped his boots in the doorway and came in. He pushed the door shut with his elbow. The ax was tucked under one arm, but both forearms were piled high with kindling. He dropped the load on the floor by Roberto.

Roberto looked up at him. "Good work. Thanks." He nodded. Then he ripped the paper from the tea tin down the middle. He crumpled half and put it inside one of the kindling pyramids. He struck a match and lit the paper.

The boy laid his ax on the table. He knelt on the floor and put his face down low and blew. He fed pieces of kindling to the fire. Roberto took a burning piece of kindling and set fire to the tinder in the other pyramids. Then he knelt beside the boy and blew like him. They blew and added kindling and blew.

A log caught fire.

Roberto stood and hung the pot of snow on the black hook over the fire. When the water boiled, he poured in a handful of buckwheat. Then another. He didn't know how much buckwheat to use. At home his mother was the cook, and all he paid attention to was the taste of things. And in the work camps one of the German soldiers had always cooked. But Roberto knew some things—he knew buckwheat swelled. Still, how big could two handfuls swell? And there was the boy to feed, as well. He threw in three more handfuls. Then he searched till he found a long-handled spoon. He stirred.

The heat from the fire made him queasy. He fell to his knees. Everything was going dark. He put both hands on the floor and dropped his head down between them. He waited. The darkness passed, and now he could hear the crackles of the fire once more. The water in the pot hissed. But Roberto didn't dare stand, for fear he might fall in the fire. He held the spoon out to the boy. "Stir."

The boy took the spoon.

Roberto lay on his back. He was suddenly too weak to even lift his head. He watched the boy stir the buckwheat and every now and then stoop and blow into the fire. It was as though Roberto were far, far away, looking on a distant scene. The boy could be a figure in a movie—a Western—they cooked over fires in the old American West—

and Roberto could be in the audience. Like in Mestre.

After a while, the room smelled hearty, as though the air itself could be eaten. "Taste it." Roberto put his hand to his mouth and gestured eating. "Is it ready?"

The boy grabbed a cloth to protect his hand and took the pot off the hook. He set it on the table, got two bowls and filled them, and handed a bowl and a wooden spoon to Roberto. His movements were smooth and competent. Roberto's chest tightened in gratitude. The boy sat at the table and ate, his eyes on Roberto.

Roberto sat up slowly and crossed his ankles. Every mouthful was wonderful. He ate as much as he could. "You cook good for an atheist," he said to the boy.

The boy looked at him solemnly.

"That's what they told us in school—that you're all atheists, all you communists. Atheists and bastards. Are you a bastard? Do you know your father?" Roberto looked at the quiet face of the boy. "None of it matters, does it?" He lay back and slept.

When he woke up, the boy was sitting in the chair asleep, his head and arms on the table. Roberto ate the rest of his buckwheat. He stood up and looked in the pot. The boy had finished it off.

Roberto went outside and filled the pot with snow again. He came back in and cooked another pot of buckwheat.

The boy woke.

"I'm still hungry. How about you?" Roberto stirred the buckwheat. "Is there anyone else alive in this village?"

The boy watched Roberto. The ax lay across his knees.

"You've given up trying to talk to me, huh? That's too bad. I'd like to hear your voice." Roberto filled both bowls and sat opposite the boy at the table. He ate.

The boy finished his buckwheat and went to a wooden box in the corner. He opened it and brought a bottle of vodka to the table.

Roberto shook his head. "No, thanks." He smiled. Then he laughed. "You don't drink that, do you?"

The boy put a glass on the table and filled it. He pushed it toward Roberto.

Roberto went to the bed. There were two pillows. He shook them out of their cases and went outside with the pillowcases tucked in his waistband. "Come on. Stick with me."

The boy followed him.

They went from house to house. In one house they found a cage with a pair of canaries, and the birds were somehow still alive. Roberto marveled at finding the yellow birds here. He knew they were native to Germany, because a friend of his mother's had a pair. The people of this house must have gotten them before the war started. Roberto picked up the heavy bag of birdseed under the cage. He

opened the cage door and scattered seeds all around the
bottom. He hooked the door so that it stayed open. Then
he scattered seeds around the house, on every surface. He
filled all the containers he could find with snow and left
them in front of the windows where the sun might melt
them. He and the boy went outside. "Good luck," he called
back into the room. Then he closed the front door to the
house tight behind them.

In another house, they found a hungry dog, skulking in
the corner. It whined. But when Roberto called to it and
stepped forward, it growled and raised a ridge of hair along
its back. So far the dog hadn't attacked the human bodies
on the floor. But, then, it had probably been only a day
since the soldiers had killed them. Soon enough the dog
would decide the bodies were meat. Roberto backed away
carefully, leaving the door ajar.

The cat that he'd seen the night before had hidden
somewhere. Roberto called for it, but it never came.

And that was the sum total of living beings in the village. If there had been cows or goats or horses, there was
no sign of them now. How had the boy survived the raid?
Maybe he'd been off somewhere doing a task. Or maybe
he'd been playing, sliding on a frozen pond, happy, and
come home too late to die.

And why had this village been so completely destroyed?
Roberto's head ached with the question. But now was

the time for action; unanswerable questions couldn't matter.

Both pillowcases were near full with the various foods and supplies that Roberto and the boy had collected from the houses. And both Roberto and the boy were now fairly well equipped. They each had a knife in their pocket. They each had on a long-sleeved shirt, two sweaters, three pairs of socks, sturdy boots, two pairs of trousers. And they had gloves, scarves, and hats.

It was midafternoon. They could get in maybe four hours of walking before dark. It wasn't enough to merit the risk.

"Let's go on back to the third house." That was the house farthest from the road, the only house without a body in it. The people must have heard the raid. Maybe they were smart and had run off into the fields and away— oh, maybe, oh, please let that be so. But maybe they had run out and met their murderers. Then their bodies would be lost in the snow somewhere. "Come on." Roberto led the way, putting his boots down gingerly, just in case. The boy followed at his heels.

They set up logs, kindling, and tinder, carefully and thoroughly. There would be no mishaps this time. And there would be no waste. Roberto had gathered all the matches and paper he could find—and he wasn't about to use any now if he didn't have to. There was no telling how long his little cache of matches and paper would have to last him. He'd been thinking about it as they went from house to house. His planning made him efficient.

Roberto walked back to the house in which they'd built the fire earlier. The coals were still hot. He laid two wet logs on the floor in front of the fireplace, then used larger kindling to sweep coals onto the wet logs. With the two logs held tightly together, he ran to the third house. He dumped the coals in the fireplace. The tinder took flame. The flame passed from one pyramid to another. Samuele would have smiled at him. Roberto basked for a moment in the glow of the imagined praise.

When Roberto was sure the fire wouldn't go out, he got up and went once more from house to house, securing the doors as best he could. He didn't know how long it might take wolves to discover the village was nothing but a heap of corpses, but he figured that if the houses were kept closed, it would take that much longer. And he needed to delay them only one night. Tomorrow Roberto and the boy would get far away from here.

The only door he didn't shut was of the house with the dog.

The boy followed him in this work. He didn't say a word. He watched everything Roberto did, every detail. And he did his part, often anticipating Roberto's next move and helping before Roberto asked. He was smart. And he was such a little kid. And his family was dead. Roberto wished they could have talked.

Roberto and the boy returned to their chosen house and watched the fire.

After a while the boy got up. He lifted a section of board from the floor and pulled out potatoes and onions from a tiny cellar. They buried them in the embers of the hearth till they were roasted through. Then they ate till they were full. Roberto roasted half of the remaining potatoes from the cellar. He packed the roasted ones plus the raw ones into the pillowcases. He put three logs on the fire. Then he took off his boots and stripped down to a single layer of clothing. He lay on the bed and pulled the quilt over himself.

"Come on, Ragazzo," said Roberto, calling him by the Italian word for "boy." "Let's sleep."

The boy stripped likewise and climbed into the wide bed beside Roberto.

"I have a story to tell you," said Roberto softly. "I don't really like this story, and since you're atheist, maybe it'll mean nothing to you, and since I'm talking Italian, surely it'll mean nothing to you. But a friend of mine told it to me and he thought it made sense. And he knew a lot more about how things work than I do. So I'll tell you now, Ragazzo. I'll tell you because I'm afraid that everyone you love is dead, and I have to try to comfort you. I have to try." Roberto whispered, "There once was a man named Job, who had seven sons and three daughters." He whispered on and on. He fell asleep whispering.

The rattle of a tin cup on a shelf woke Roberto. He leaped up. Morning rays shot through the windows. A cat sat on the shelf and looked at him. "Meow."

"How did you get in here?" Roberto walked around the house, looking everywhere. There were no openings he could make out, no drafts coming from secret holes. He jumped back on the bed and rubbed his feet—the floor was cold. He pulled the quilt up around his shoulders. The air was cold, too.

The boy was awake by now. He got up and petted the cat, showing no signs of surprise at its appearance and no discomfort at the cold in the house.

Roberto stretched. "Is it yours?"

The boy looked at him.

Roberto pulled on another layer of clothing. He got out of bed and jabbed at the fireplace with a shovel. There were a few live coals still. He fed them tinder and kindling. Then he put on the rest of his clothes, and he pulled on his boots. He went outside and fetched logs. It had snowed again during the night, like clockwork. Roberto went back into the house and slowly, slowly got the fire roaring. He poured the last of some dry oats into a pot of boiling water, then sweetened the hot breakfast mash with sugar lumps he'd taken from another house. Such a little thing, making breakfast. Yet Roberto felt distinctly proud of his resourcefulness. He could do this. He could take care of himself and this boy.

The boy produced a brown bread from a cloth bag. It was hard, but not rock hard. He sawed off a few slices and warmed them near the fire. They were good.

"What else can you find stashed around these houses?" Roberto picked up a pillowcase. He held it open before the boy. "We've got to put whatever we can into these. We're going to need it. Is there anything else you haven't told me about?" He shook the pillowcase.

The boy just looked at him.

Roberto made a tsking noise. There was nothing left to do. He wished he could have found himself an overcoat. The boy had one. But there were none left in any of the houses—none except children's, which were too small for Roberto. The soldiers must have taken them. Probably the Italian soldiers.

Roberto took one last look around the room. He picked up two tin cups and put them into the pillowcases. Then he tied the top of each case closed. He handed the lighter one to the boy. "Come on."

They walked outside. The new snow had covered their footprints from the searchings yesterday. But it had also covered the soldiers' footprints, so that Roberto couldn't follow their trail anymore. That was okay. They'd just go south. And if they met any obstacles, they'd go west.

He walked ahead on out of town.

The boy stopped. He yanked on Roberto's arm urgently. Then he handed Roberto his pillowcase and ran back toward the houses.

"Stop," called Roberto. He dropped both pillowcases and ran after the boy. "You can't stay here. You won't survive alone."

The boy disappeared behind a house.

And now doubt hit Roberto hard in the chest. The boy had to know how far it was to the next bit of civilization. Maybe he knew that heading out on their own was sure death. Maybe he knew about something horrible in the wilds. The image of a photograph in an old school textbook came to him vividly: a big brown Russian bear. Maybe there were bears in Ukraine, too. Did brown bears eat people?

Maybe their only chance was to stay here and wait for help. But then more soldiers might come. No wild animal could compare to soldiers. Roberto turned the corner of the house.

The boy smiled at him. He lifted a small sled off big iron hooks that stuck out from the side of the house.

"Fantastic!" Roberto hugged him. "You're wonderful." He went into that house and took the pillows, the quilt, a pot, bowls, spoons. He came out and piled a layer of firewood on the sled. Then the extra provisions. He pulled the sled out to the place where they'd left the pillowcases. He put the pillowcases on top, using his potato-sack blanket to cover the whole thing. Then he tied it all up tight with his rope.

"Meow." The cat stood in the snow.

The boy picked up the cat and put it on top of the pile. He looked at Roberto with big, defiant eyes.

Roberto nodded. If the boy wanted the cat, that was fine with him.

The boy turned around and ran back to another house.

Roberto waited. He didn't care how much time the boy took; whatever he brought back was bound to be worth the wait.

The boy was gone a long while. He came out the door carrying something big and square wrapped up several times in a quilt.

Roberto ran to help him carry it. But the load was amazingly light. "What is it?"

The boy flapped his arms.

Roberto gaped. "You caught the canaries? How are we going to attach a birdcage to the sled?"

But the boy had already produced a rope and was going to work.

"The birds will die in this cold."

The boy tied the cage to the top of it all, leaving room enough for the cat to sit beside it. He lashed the ax to the side.

So they marched out of the village: two doomed canaries in a cage in a quilt, one orange and brown cat perched on the pillowcases, and two boys bundled up so much that they waddled.

Roberto looked back over his shoulder, expecting to see the whining dog.

And he wasn't disappointed.

THE SLED

The dog had to be coaxed to eat potatoes. But the boy was patient, and in the end he prevailed.

Roberto forced himself to keep quiet about the food. After all, without the boy, they wouldn't have any potatoes at all. So if he wanted to share them with the dog—and the cat, too, but the cat ate less—it wasn't Roberto's right to object. Survival came at different costs for different people. And some costs were too high to pay. The boy wouldn't abandon the animals even if it meant less food for him. What wouldn't Roberto do?

They covered a good distance; Roberto was sure of that. The land started out gently rolling. It was just past the first little knoll that Roberto and the boy passed the German jeep. Even with the layer of snow on it, even with pieces exploded off, even all charred, it was immediately recognizable. The villagers must have set a mine in the road. Four German soldiers had been killed, their bodies strewn helter-skelter. But the rest of the force had passed on. The villagers had paid dearly for that jeep and those four soldiers.

Roberto and the boy looked at the jeep, but they didn't stop moving. They walked and walked. The path was distinctly downhill now, and the snow was only a thumb deep, if that. The wind was always behind them, which helped, too. They didn't talk, but now and then the boy sang, his voice muffled in the scarf across his chin and mouth. His songs and eyes were without a trace of happiness—Roberto knew he sang just to keep his mind occupied. Maybe to keep from thinking about his lost village.

They came to a stand of woods in early afternoon, and their going slowed down. The floor of the grove had very little snow, for the thick branches had kept it out, along with most of the sunlight. But in its place was ice. Melting snow dripped from the top branches and froze when it reached the dark ground.

Pulling the sled was harder now, too. It snagged on icy roots and low branches. Sometimes the underbrush was so thick they had to make detours. It was close to evening by the time they emerged from the woods. The clearing in front of them seemed endless. And it was obviously warmer here than the land on the other side of the woods had been because most of the snow had melted away, leaving only scattered white patches.

Roberto took a few steps out into the clearing. The ground was soft. Over to the east side, bulrushes and cattails waved in the slight breeze. This land was almost marsh. It would be hard to cross. His heart sank.

"Let's camp here for the night." Roberto pulled the sled back to the woods' edge and tied it to the trunk of a thin pine sapling.

The boy shook his head.

"It could be a long way till we get to trees again. And if we're out in the open, the wind will chill us. It's a breeze now, but it could pick up. And snow could fall again. And anyone who came along might see us." Roberto unlashed the ax as he talked. He cut down the lower branches of a pine. "Anyway, the ground is all marshy. We'll face it tomorrow—after a good night's sleep. I'll tell you another bedtime story. How does that sound?" He turned around.

The boy had untied the sled and pulled it out into the clearing.

"Hey!" Roberto ran after him. He grabbed him by the arm. "It's safer in the woods." He looked at the boy's silent, firm face. "Really. I know."

The boy pulled his arm away. He gestured that they should go forward, across the clearing.

Roberto snatched the pull rope of the sled. "I'm exhausted. I've been traveling longer than you. I've been traveling for days." He wanted to use a coaxing voice, but he was too tired to manage anything but plain words. "We'll cross the clearing in the morning."

"*Khody! Tse nedaleko,*" said the boy. He stamped his foot.

Roberto shook his head. "No. We're staying here."

The boy reached for the rope.

Roberto held it behind his back. "No!" He pulled the sled back to the tree. He tied it again. He turned and faced the boy. "We'll build a fire and eat. And then we'll tell stories. And then we'll sleep."

The boy walked over slowly. His shoulders slumped.

Roberto used a cut branch to sweep away snow and leave a circle of exposed earth. What next? The branches he had cut off were green. The dead branches on the floor of the grove were soaked through. He had no kindling, and the logs on the sled wouldn't start without lots of kindling—he'd learned that lesson already.

Well, then, he'd find a tree with dead branches still attached. That way they'd be dry. Maybe he'd even find a whole dead tree still standing. Back at the last work camp, the boys learned to tell a dead tree from a live one even after the leaves had fallen off, just by knocking on the wood and listening. Samuele had been the one to teach them.

He'd read about it in his nature books, of course. Roberto smiled to himself; Samuele was still helping him, even now. He picked up the ax. "We need dry wood. Want to come?"

The boy stared at him.

Roberto didn't want to leave the sled there, where the boy might try to take off with it again. But he couldn't very well pull it behind him as he searched for dry wood. And, anyway, he'd be back soon. The boy couldn't get far, especially since it would be hard to pull the sled across mud. Still, Roberto went to the tree and tied a harder knot in the sled rope. "I'll be right back. Stay here, okay? Don't act crazy."

He set off into the woods. But it was later than he'd thought, and evening came swiftly, adding to the natural dark of the trees. He knocked on trunk after trunk, limb after limb, listening for the hollow sound of dead wood. By this time, he could hardly see. Without a single branch, he headed back for the edge of the woods.

They didn't really need a fire, after all. The pillowcases were full of food in jars, food that was already cooked— meat and vegetables and even fruits, from the looks of them. So they didn't have to cook. And they had good clothes, plus the potato-sack blanket and the quilts. They'd be warm enough without a fire.

Roberto walked through the woods. He should have been at the clearing by now. He must have gotten turned around. He called out, "Ragazzo! Where are you, Ragazzo?" No answer. But the boy might not answer even if Roberto was only ten meters from him.

He went faster. Now he ran, stumbling over roots. He slammed into branches. "Ragazzo!" He tried to get a view of the sky that might orient him, but the trees were too thick. Anyway, he didn't know enough about the stars. "Ragazzo!" He fell. Stabbing pains cut through his right knee. He got up and ran again.

And suddenly he burst out onto the clearing. He limped along the edge of the woods, searching for the boy and the sled. And then he spied the tracks of the sled in the hardening mud; they were just visible in the early moonlight. He looked out where they led, but he couldn't see anyone. He cupped his hands around his mouth and shouted, "Ragazzo!"

He slapped one fist into his palm in frustration. He had been stupid to leave the boy alone with the sled. Stupid stupid. And he was even stupider now to call out to him. Voices in the night air carry far—who knew what ears that one word would reach? He should turn around, go back and climb a tree, wait for morning. But the thought of spending another night alone in the wild undid him.

And what if the boy got so far away Roberto couldn't find him again? Everything Roberto needed was on that sled.

Roberto followed the runner tracks. The ground had hardened enough with the progressing night cold that he could walk across it easily, after all. Maybe that's why the boy had gone ahead—because he knew the morning sun would make the crossing more difficult.

Soon the ground got fully solid and the tracks disappeared. Roberto strained his eyes in the moonlight. Which way? Which way? And there they were again—runner tracks visible in a patch of snow ahead. Roberto moved quickly. He wouldn't allow himself to limp and he wouldn't think about what else might be wandering in the night. He stood tall and walked and walked and walked. He was hungry, he was tired, he was angry. The boy should have waited for him out here. Roberto would have waited for the boy.

Then the air changed somehow. It wasn't that he heard anything really, yet he knew there was something in the air. He stared ahead and saw the outlines of the town. This was bigger than his boy's settlement, much bigger; there were buildings standing large in the night and roads and lights in houses and the feel of motors in the air—that was it—the tiny rumbles of all those things that go into making homes light up and factories run. Smoke puffed out of chimneys.

This town was alive. The German and Italian soldiers had not passed this way. No one waged war here. The world was suddenly familiar again. Familiar and wonderful.

Roberto ran toward the lights. He tripped and fell face forward onto a log. He got to his knees and felt around. A series of logs with a long strip of metal. It was tracks. Train tracks.

Roberto stood. Thank heavens for these tracks. They'd stopped him from his rash race to the town. What had he been thinking? This was Ukraine. He was Italian. His people were at war with these people, whether there were battles in this town or not. He had to go carefully, or he'd wind up a prisoner of war.

He looked up and down the train tracks. They ran almost due south—the same direction he'd been walking. He might have been parallel to these tracks all along. Why hadn't he heard a train go by?

He stepped from tie to tie, and within minutes the answer came: He stood on the edge of a ditch. Someone had dug it deep and very steep at the edges. The tracks broke off here and picked up several meters away, on the other side. Why? Did the Germans and Italians do it to cut the town off from supplies? Or did the townsfolk do it to keep the invaders from coming in by train?

Roberto's skin prickled. Either way, this town was part of the war.

He left the tracks and walked along the edge of the ditch. Why such a long ditch? It wasn't just to stop the train. He thought back to the soldiers—the straggling line of tired men, the mules, the tanks. That was it: the tanks. Tanks couldn't get across this ditch.

Roberto climbed down into the ditch. As he climbed out the other side, he heard something. He listened hard. Yes, he heard it for sure. There was water here. A river. He ran directly for it. That's when he saw the runner tracks again. The boy and the sled and the dog had passed by here. How did they cross the ditch? Where?

Roberto followed the runner tracks. They didn't go toward the water. And they didn't go down toward the road Roberto could make out now, where a lone truck rolled along. They went straight to a house at the edge of town.

Roberto stood with the ax over his shoulder and surveyed the scene. There was nothing special about the house his boy's tracks led to. But the house beside it had a stable out back. Roberto could sleep there with the animals. Then he could rise before dawn and, with a clear head, figure out what to do next.

He hunched over and walked as fast as he could toward the stable.

A shout came. He ran. The crack of a gun split the air. He fell.

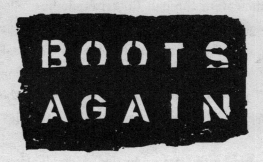

BOOTS AGAIN

The pain in Roberto's arm raged like fire. He sat naked on a wooden chair by the wall. He did his best to relax his whole body. When he was little and about to get his smallpox vaccination, Sergio had told him that if he relaxed, it would hurt less. Sergio said that was true about all pain. It seemed right. The pain was slowly transforming into a steady ache. If he relaxed more, maybe he wouldn't feel it at all.

His boy lay asleep on a couch nearby. He was curled on his side, and he looked younger than ever. Yet he'd managed to get here from the grove by himself. And he'd found a way to cross that ditch with the sled. There was no telling what he could do.

And there was no telling what he had already done. Had he told about Roberto? Was he responsible for Roberto's getting shot?

Two men went through Roberto's clothes, piled on the table. They argued over his German boots. They looked at him and barked questions. Roberto didn't speak—not a word. He knew that his boy had no idea what language he spoke. So if he kept his mouth shut now, maybe no one would realize he was on the other side—that he was the enemy.

The kettle on the stove whistled. A dog howled. Roberto hadn't noticed it before. It was the dog from his boy's village, the potato eater. It came out from under the couch and howled at the kettle. The canaries in the cage on the floor beside the couch made little peeping screeches and hopped from perch to perch. They had actually survived the day, protected by nothing but a few layers of quilt. Roberto's eyes searched the room for the cat. It was nowhere in sight. That didn't surprise him; that was the cat's trick.

A woman came into the room. This house was larger than the houses back at his boy's village. It had at least two rooms. The woman poured the hot water from the kettle into a pottery basin painted with a profusion of red and yellow flowers. The embroidered throw on the back of the couch was bright, too—red and blue animals ran among flowers. And the braided rug on the floor by the table was red and black and blue and yellow. Even the stove was painted with flowers. The room would have been cheerful if Roberto was just a friend stopping by. He'd have been happy to be here.

The woman dropped a knife into the hot water in the basin. Then she picked up a small towel in one hand and a bottle of vodka in the other.

She came over to Roberto. She said something.

Roberto stared at the basin. She had dropped a knife in the water. A knife. Now he looked at the vodka. He thought of how his boy offered him vodka. He thought of how the two German soldiers at the work camp had died after drinking vodka. These people seemed half mad, to drink something so strong. The very smell of it made him woozy. But there was the knife. Maybe being drunk right now would be a good idea. Then he remembered vomiting after the grappa episode on Memo's birthday. He shook his head.

The woman didn't seem to notice his shaking head. She took his left arm by the elbow. She raised the bottle and poured vodka onto his wound.

The dull ache turned to searing pain. Roberto pulled his arm away.

The woman went back to the basin and fished out the knife with a wooden spoon. She came back and grabbed his elbow firmly.

Roberto looked away.

He felt the knife jab. He let out a yelp. The bullet dropped with a small clunk on the wooden floor. Then came the searing pain again, as the vodka rolled down his arm. And finally the woman wrapped it tight in a strip of white cloth. She tied it in place with a smaller strip.

Roberto wiped the tears from his cheeks. As the woman turned away, he took her skirt with his right hand. She looked at him. He pulled her as close as he could. His arm hurt so bad. But his gut hurt, too. He gestured eating. He pressed on his stomach. Anyone could understand hunger.

The woman hesitated. Her face was drawn; she was bone thin. She knew hunger—Roberto could see that plainly in her face. Her head tilted in a small, tired gesture of pity.

Then her eyes changed. With a sudden fierceness, she yanked her skirt free and went to the table. She talked to the men without looking at Roberto.

The language was gibberish to Roberto, of course. But he read the people's faces, their shoulders, their pointing fingers. Everything seemed to come back to those German boots. And now one man went over to the sled that sat by the front door. It had been untied, and the various provisions from the pillowcases stood against the far wall. He picked up the potato-sack blanket and carried it to the table. The three of them talked and pointed at the German words printed on it and looked at Roberto and talked some more.

So they thought he was a German soldier. He should have thrown away the potato sack and, especially, those boots. After all, they'd been the cause of Samuele's death. He should have stripped boots off a corpse in his boy's village. He hadn't thought to do it—probably because he didn't want to touch the bodies. But, oh, he hated those German boots. And he didn't want anyone to think he was a soldier.

But what difference did it make really? Whether he was a soldier or just a worker—it didn't matter. He was the enemy. The fascist. He'd built the pen the Polish girl sat in all day. He'd built airstrips in two different places so that German planes could bomb Soviet towns. He was the enemy.

These people could argue all night. But Roberto couldn't listen to them all night. He got off the chair and lay on the floor.

One of the men came over and pulled him to his feet. He handed him his clothes—all but the boots.

Roberto got dressed. It hurt to pull the sweaters over his left arm. It scared him to look at the crusted blood on the wool of the sleeve where he'd been shot. Was he bleeding right now through the bandage the woman had put on his arm? And it hurt to use that arm to pull up his trousers. Yet an unexpected gratitude overwhelmed him. He felt thick and warm and, despite the pain, oddly safe in those peasant clothes.

The man tied Roberto's hands behind his back. He tied his ankles. He said something.

Roberto lay down on the floor again. He curled his back toward his knees, as though to squeeze away the pain.

Somewhere in the back of his head the image of a hunch-back shimmered. Was it Samuele? Was it Roberto himself?

Then he was instantly asleep.

When he woke, the room was full of men wearing small caps and muttering to one another. Roberto was sweaty and stiff. The house was tightly made, and a fire had been going all night. He shouldn't have slept fully dressed.

One of the men from last night saw him wake. He untied Roberto and let him relieve himself in a chamber pot. Then he sat him at the table and put a bowl in front of him.

Roberto snaked his hands into his pockets and waited for someone to fill the bowl. That's when he realized his pockets were empty. He looked around the room. The things from his pockets lay in a small pile on the floor by the other provisions from the sled. Roberto jumped up and leaped for the pile. His fingers closed over the Polish girl's gift stone as one of the men grabbed his arm. His left arm. He let out a cry of pain and clutched the stone to his chest.

The man pushed him back into his chair. And all the men were talking at once. They forced his hand open and examined the stone and talked. Then the man put the stone on the table.

Roberto snatched it back. He looked from one man to the next. It was just a stone. They could see it was just a stone.

The men talked. One of them yelled at him sharply.

His boy woke up. A man said something to him. The boy cried out happily and ran to the table. The man put a bowl in front of him, too. Then the man poured from a pitcher into both bowls.

The smell of goat soaked the air and rushed up Roberto's nose. Steamy, foaming goat milk filled his bowl. Roberto stared in delight; he hadn't expected goats in this flat country. The man gave each boy a large hunk of bread. Roberto didn't need a second invitation. He put the stone in his pocket and ripped off pieces of the bread. He dunked them in the goat milk and ate as fast as he could. It was delicious.

The men tried talking gently to him now. One of them spoke a few words of German. Roberto worked to keep his eyes dull. He prayed that his boy wouldn't remember when he'd said that single German word to him—*Wasser*. He looked quickly at him. The boy just ate.

Another man tried garbled Italian. Roberto's heart sped. He concentrated on eating. He refused to look at his boy. But now the man was saying the word for "boy." The boy had to recognize it; it was what Roberto called him.

The boy stood up. Roberto almost gagged on his bread. The boy took the pitcher of goat milk and refilled his own bowl. Then he refilled Roberto's. He went back to eating, making loud slurping sounds.

Roberto looked at the full bowl in front of him. It wasn't an accident. He was sure his boy had filled the bowl at that very moment to show he recognized Roberto's language. Did that mean he'd stand by him—he wouldn't give him away? Or did that mean he'd blackmail him, like the food thief blackmailed Samuele back at the farm work camp?

Another man tried some other language on Roberto— something odd that Roberto felt sure he'd never heard before.

Roberto looked at them with a blank face, eating steadily. He finished his bread. He drank the remaining milk in the bowl and licked it clean. He was full and satisfied. He was ready to face anything. He looked at the men with clear eyes. He would wait them out. They would have to decide what to do with him without knowing anything about him.

Their decision came swiftly. They tied his hands behind him and slapped his hat on his head. They put his boots in front of him.

Roberto refused to step into the boots. Soldier boots.

The men talked about this, too. Then one of them pushed him to the ground. Pain shot up his left arm. He groaned. The man jammed the boots onto Roberto's feet.

They pushed him out the door. The morning air was mild, with hardly a breeze. Roberto shuffled down a street,

around a corner, pushed, always pushed, by the hands of
a half-dozen men. He moved through fog so thick, he could
hardly see the ground beneath his feet. It was as though
he walked in clouds. Most of the buildings were abandoned. Had the German and Italian soldiers made it past
the ditch, after all? But none of the doors Roberto passed
were bashed in. No windows that he could see were broken. Something had happened to this town, but it didn't
look like war or like what Roberto knew of war. These
buildings gave the sense of having been abandoned for
years.

They walked down another street, around another corner. Then they opened a door and pushed Roberto into
what was clearly an official building. They stepped into a
foyer, practically filling it. They pounded on the door on
the right. It opened and a somewhat stupefied man stood
back as they all poured into that office.

When the talking was over, Roberto was left sitting in
a chair, his arms tied behind him and around the chair
back, so that he couldn't get up. The man whose office it
was sat behind the desk. And the other men had finally
been persuaded to go on their way.

The man at the desk said something. He got up and
walked around Roberto. He pointed at the hateful boots.
He sat at the desk again.

Roberto's boy came in. He talked to the man. The man

talked and talked. The boy looked long at Roberto. He left.

Maybe the town was too small to have a jail. Or maybe prisoners of war weren't put in the jail. Roberto wiggled his hands. The rope was tight. His left arm throbbed now. And his right knee, the one he'd slammed on the ground yesterday evening as he raced through the woods, hurt again.

But at least he wasn't cold. The office had no source of heat, so Roberto's layers of clothes served him well. And the hat had little flaps that covered his ears. They felt good.

The man cleared his throat. He spoke again, but this time his voice was different. He wasn't asking questions or scolding. He was just talking. He sounded sad. Then he fell silent. He put his elbows on the desk and dropped his head in his palms.

There were knocks on the door. A group of women came in with one of the men from this morning. Every single women wore a kerchief on her head with a part in her hair showing at the forehead. It was like a school dress code—a uniform. And now Roberto noticed: All these women were bone thin, like the woman who'd cut out his bullet. And the men he'd seen were thin, too. Snippets of old newsreels about famine in Ukraine came rushing into Roberto's head. That was years ago. These people had been hungry for years.

The women looked at Roberto while the man talked on and on to them. There was no animus in their faces. There wasn't much of anything except a worried curiosity. They left.

Roberto yawned. The man at the desk looked at him and yawned, too. He stood and hitched up his loose trousers at the waist. He said something. Then he went out through a back door. He came back a few moments later, stretched, and sat down again.

A group of children filed into the room and looked at Roberto in silence. Their faces were round, even over their stick-thin bodies. Their eyes were brown. They could have been children anywhere—children in Venice or in the streets of Munich or in the pen of Polish Jews. After a while the man shooed the children out.

A long period passed again. Roberto felt stiff all over. He pushed his legs out full length and wiggled his toes inside his boots. The man glanced at him. The skin on his knee tightened. A scab had formed over the spot where he'd hurt himself yesterday. How long would it take for a scab to form over the bullet hole in his arm?

His boy came in holding a sweet bun bigger than both his hands. Roberto looked at it in amazement. So did the man. It was clear the boy held a treasure. He talked to the man, who licked his bottom lip several times. The boy sniffed loudly at the bun every so often as he talked. Why didn't he just take a huge bite? That's what Roberto wanted to do. Gobble it up.

Roberto's stomach growled. The boy and the man looked over at him. The boy left.

The man said a few words to Roberto. He pulled a watch from his pocket and glanced at it. It had to be past noon—it was definitely lunchtime. The man walked behind Roberto and checked the knot that held his wrists together. He rested his hand softly on Robert's head for an instant. Then he bolted the office door from the inside and went out through the back door.

Within seconds, the back door reopened. His boy ran in, holding peasant boots under his arm. In one hand was a hunting knife. Roberto jerked himself to attention. Every muscle tensed. The boy put the boots on the floor and ran behind Roberto. He sawed at the ropes on Roberto's wrists till they split.

Roberto stood up. He was free.

The boy jammed the peasant boots into Roberto's stomach. *"Skoro! Bizhy!"* He ran out the door, holding the knife.

Roberto clutched the boots, dumbfounded. Then he raced after the boy. They went through a small room with a chamber pot in one corner and out another door to the outside. They were behind the building now, in a bare courtyard that several other buildings backed onto. The sun had burned off the fog, and the surfaces of everything glistened. The boy hissed something and pointed at the boots. He was right, of course. Roberto sat on the ground and pulled off the German boots. He put on the peasant ones. Now he looked just like any other Ukrainian kid.

The boy stuffed Roberto's old boots into a crate behind the building next door. He pulled a roll from his pocket, dropped it in Roberto's lap, and ran between two buildings.

Roberto ran after him. But no one was between the buildings. His boy had disappeared. No. He couldn't have deserted him so soon. Roberto needed him to escape. He needed him.

Roberto ran to the front of the buildings and stopped. He peeked out at the street. It was empty. Lunchtime. Every last soul was off eating. He came out from the alley and ran down the block, looking around wildly for his boy.

A door opened ahead of him.

Roberto ducked between two buildings.

He heard men talking. Their voices got closer. He crouched and turned his back on them. He felt like he was going to choke. The voices and footsteps passed.

Roberto stood up. He realized he was still clutching the roll his boy had given him. He took a big bite and peeked at the road. A man came out of that same door, crossed the street, and got into a small truck. The sides were wooden slats connected together with steel cords. One of the slats was broken, and Roberto could see that the bed of the truck was empty.

A surge of energy filled him. Could he climb into the back of the truck without the driver seeing him?

The truck drove off.

Roberto clenched his teeth. He had to be faster in taking whatever opportunities came up. He had to be fast like his boy. Fast like Memo and Sergio.

Another truck was parked behind where the first one had been. An identical truck. Roberto couldn't see into the back of it. It might be completely full—with no room at all for a stowaway. He looked up and down the road. Nothing else seemed to offer even the smallest hint of a promise. He had to chance it.

He dashed across the street and climbed into the back of the truck. It was blessedly empty. He lay flat on the wooden bottom. He didn't even dare to finish the roll clutched in his right hand. Anyone who looked in the back of the truck could see him. Anyone. He heard a door slam. Then footsteps. Roberto's breathing was too loud. He held his breath. The footsteps stopped. A voice called out.

Another voice answered. And someone ran toward the truck.

Roberto flattened his palms on the truck bed, letting go of the roll. There was nothing to hold on to. He had the unbearable sensation of falling.

The truck doors slammed. Both of them, one after the

other. The truck engine revved up, and it rolled down the street.

Roberto found he was panting. The sun was high. He squinted his eyes against it. The truck turned, and he slid. He clanked against the truck side—oh, no—he was sure the people in the truck cab had heard. But the truck didn't stop. It went slowly through the streets. Roberto felt around for the roll. He found it and ate. He was grateful the buildings were only one story high—no one could just happen to look out an upper window and see a boy in the back of a truck stuffing bread into his mouth. He would make it out of town.

But the truck turned another corner and stopped abruptly.

UNDER BUSHES

Roberto heard two people get out of the front of the truck. One of them walked around and opened the back.

Roberto sat up.

The old man blinked his eyes in surprise. Then he shooed him away.

Roberto bolted over the side of the truck and ran past the other man, who was kneeling by a front wheel. Roberto saw the river at the end of the road. He ran straight for it.

The men shouted. Their voices were startled. Roberto heard running.

He left the road and ducked into the trees that flanked both sides of the river. He ran. Pain pounded in his left arm. He held it across his chest. The running behind him got closer.

He went down to the bushes at the water's edge. He stumbled and crawled far under a bush and cracked his head hard against something. Wet stuff ran down the bridge of his nose. He wiped it away—blood. He let himself drop so that he lay flat on the ground, dizzy, aching in his arm, his knee, and now the top of his head. He shut his eyes. Lights danced behind his eyelids. He opened them and looked at the dirt. Nausea rose in his throat. He couldn't let himself vomit now. They'd hear. He put both hands over his mouth and tried to steady his stomach.

He heard the men run past.

He waited.

After a while, he heard them talking. Their voices got louder. They passed by again, close this time—very, very close. They kept walking, back to the road.

Roberto felt around under the bush. The thing he had bashed his head against moved when he pushed it. It was wooden. His groping hand closed over an open edge. His heart beat hard with rising hope. He worked his way out from under the bushes, pulling the wooden thing behind him.

It was a boat.

Roberto let his breath out in relief. He knew nothing really about how to fend off wild animals or how to stay warm in snow. But he knew about boats—oh, yes, he knew about boats.

The boat was barely his body's length and only three times his width at the center. It had no seat. Roberto crawled back under the bushes and felt around. He grabbed a paddle. There was only one.

He quickly eased the boat into the water, crunching through the last bits of thin ice that hadn't yet broken up at the very edge. He stood to paddle like in a gondola, but the handle of the paddle was too short. He had to kneel to make it work. It was tempting to hug the shore, so that he would run less of a risk of being seen. But he didn't know if the men would come back in an instant with more men. So he let the current carry him to the center of the river where the water ran the fastest.

He paddled like mad, skimming the top of the water. The river was shallow at this time of year. Bigger boats could never pass. Good—that meant he wasn't likely to meet others on the water. If only no one followed.

He didn't rest till late afternoon. He must have covered a good forty or fifty kilometers, and he'd seen no villages at all. Once he saw a few long-legged animals in the distance, maybe mules. They must have been out to pasture, but there weren't any people in sight. And once he saw a windmill. That's all.

The river ran through a gently sloping, broad valley. Meadows filled huge depressions. There was no snow here, though the air wasn't much warmer than back in his boy's settlement. The grasses were dry yellow. On the west bank he passed a dirt road that ran from the river's edge to a wooded area in the distance. It looked like it had been lumberjacked. He knew that way beyond the woods rose the white-capped Carpathians, but he couldn't see that far.

Roberto was hungry, but just being on the water kept him calm. He sat in the bottom of the boat and stretched his legs. He thought over the past few days. He'd walked for three days before he found his boy. Taking off for the fact that sometimes he'd gone southeast instead of due south, he figured he must have traveled fifty kilometers southward each day. Maybe a bit less because he'd walked in snow some of the time, and he'd stopped to watch the soldiers pass. So maybe he averaged forty kilometers a day. That made one hundred and twenty kilometers. Then he walked one full day with his boy and most of that night alone—all of it almost directly south. So add on at least another sixty—to make one hundred and eighty kilometers. Plus this afternoon in the boat. That made a grand total of two hundred and twenty to two hundred and thirty, at a conservative estimate. It couldn't be that much farther to the Black Sea.

He pulled off his right glove and let his hand hang over the edge so that his fingertips played in the snow-fed water. He wasn't afraid of getting cold. The sun would last another few hours; the river flowed south—southeast. Things were going well for the moment.

He thought about the hot goat milk at breakfast and about the roll his boy gave him. It seemed hunger was the plague of his life. But the roll had taken off the edge; he'd been much hungrier than this before. And he'd be much hungrier again. He resisted the temptation to stop and search for food. He had to be patient and do things in the right order. He was traveling well now. He should keep traveling. So long as he was on water, he had nothing to fear.

But he did need a rest if he was going to travel well. So he let himself drift.

A small house came into view on the east shore. And another beyond it. Roberto's mouth went dry. He put on his glove, got to his knees, and paddled for the opposite shore.

A shout came across the water.

Roberto looked in panic. Two small boys waved at him from the shore. Their faces wore wide grins. Roberto swallowed his fear. He was dressed totally in peasant clothes; he could be a Ukrainian boy himself. He waved back.

The boys waved until he was out of sight.

Roberto paddled slowly now. The village was small, and of the houses Roberto could see, maybe half were abandoned. Like in the big town. What was going on?

A woman stood at the shore with a small herd of goats.

Roberto didn't hesitate this time. He waved wildly at her. She stared at him. He grinned and kept waving. Then he paddled furiously.

The village was behind him now. He looked over his shoulder. No little boats had slid into the water; no one followed.

He paddled all the rest of the day. The wind blew from the south now—a wet, heavy wind. He felt he recognized it. Was it wind off salt water? Was it, already?

Roberto passed another settlement, no larger than his boy's, without seeing a soul. A road ran through the settlement and off over a hill in one direction and then along the side of the river to the south. But Roberto was lucky—the road had no traffic.

Up ahead a bridge crossed the river. Another small settlement appeared. Roberto paddled steadily, alert and ready.

He passed under the bridge. The road went through the village and continued south. Both road and water were still untraveled. The river widened with each passing kilometer. Roberto stayed in the center.

A half-hour later, Roberto came to another town—always on the east bank. This one was big—about the size of the town that he'd spent the night in last night. And it was much busier. And what was that? The road along the river was piled high with sandbags—higher than a man's height. Roberto remembered the soldier at the farm camp laughing at how the Soviets hid behind sandbags. These people were ready for battle. If they saw Roberto on the river, they might not wait for him to wave. They might shoot on sight.

Roberto quickly paddled over to the opposite bank and hugged the shore, staying in the shadows of the trees as the sun set. The foliage was dense, and with luck he wouldn't be seen.

There were boats on the town bank. Large ones. The river had turned markedly deeper. Of course: This town was a port. Roberto dipped his hand in the water and tasted: It wasn't very salty, not like the Adriatic Sea off of Venice, but it was seawater, for sure. Roberto had finally arrived at his first goal—the Black Sea. It should be a moment for celebration—but his mind couldn't savor the victory. It spun on.

What next? He needed a plan. When he'd first thought this all through, he'd imagined walking the whole coast of the Black Sea. But he had the boat now. If he stayed close to shore, he'd be safer in the boat than walking. And even with the waves of the sea, it would be a lot faster. No matter what, he'd arrive at the strait through Turkey to the Mediterranean Sea within a week—or ten days, at the very most.

The Mediterranean Sea. His own Mediterranean Sea. The thought made his throat thick with longing. It was far—from here all the way to Venice had to be close to two thousand kilometers as the bird flies. Going by water, staying close to the shore, it could be double that. Triple maybe.

But he could do it. So long as he stayed on water, he could do it.

Roberto climbed onto the shore and pulled the boat behind him. He pushed it under bushes. Then he turned it upside down. He would sleep under the boat. He got down on his knees and started to crawl under the bushes. That's when he felt a blow across the back of his neck.

FEVER

Roberto fell on his chest and
rolled quickly to the right, kicking out his legs in defense.

"Damn!" The soldier who stood over him pointed a pistol. And he was wearing an Italian uniform. Italian! He looked quickly back at the river, then at Roberto again. "What's the matter with you people?" he hissed. "That whack was hard enough to knock any normal person out. Is a bullet the only thing that stops you? Does everything have to be death? I'm sick of you. I'm so sick of all of you." He shook his pistol as he talked, and he kept looking over his shoulder at the river every few seconds.

Roberto put his hands in the air and backed up. He kept his eyes on the pistol, but his mind raced. The man was definitely Italian. Roman, in fact. Roberto recognized his dialect from the radio. And he realized with surprise that he understood it much better now than he ever had before—a benefit of the work camps.

What was an Italian soldier doing here in the bushes?

The Roman shook his head. "A kid." He looked at the river one more time, and Roberto dared to lift his eyes from the pistol and study the man. He was in his mid-twenties, short and slight, with a black stubble of a beard. His army jacket had a long rust-colored stain down one arm, and his cuff was ripped. His eyes moved back to Roberto, and Roberto's eyes returned instantly to the pistol. "A kid all alone." The words came out in a single loud breath, as though finally exhaling after being underwater a long time. He sat on the ground and kept shaking his head. "What am I supposed to do now?"

The Roman spoke as if Roberto could understand him. Roberto had a tremendous urge to speak back, to finally be understood, to ask for help. But he forced himself to stay silent. It was better that the Roman thought he was a local. Who knew what he'd do to Roberto if he understood that Roberto had run away from the work camp? This way Roberto could listen if the Roman kept speaking his thoughts—he could be a step ahead. He could take care of himself.

The Roman's eyes moved jerkily; the bags under them were dark and deep. His stomach growled loudly. He leaned over, his pistol still pointed at Roberto, and pulled a duffel bag out from under a bush. With his left hand he fumbled around inside and produced a can. He set the pistol on his thigh and glowered at Roberto as if to say he could grab it in two seconds if Roberto dared to move. Then he opened the can by twisting a metal key. The smell of sardines filled the air. He ate with his fingers right out of the can.

Roberto stared openmouthed at the fish. The thick odor coated his tongue. The oil glistened.

The Roman wiped his mouth with the back of his hand. His eyes flicked across Roberto's face. He paused a moment and knitted his brows. Then he took out another can and threw it to Roberto.

Roberto caught it in amazed gratitude. He clutched it to his chest, afraid for a moment that the soldier would think better of it and snatch back the precious food. But the soldier wasn't even looking at the can—his eyes moved nervously from Roberto to the bushes to the river and back to Roberto. Still, Roberto had been with soldiers enough to know that food was always in short supply. He almost said *grazie*. He bit the inside of his cheek to remind himself not to talk.

Roberto took off his gloves and shoved them in his pocket. He nodded his thanks and ate. When he finished, he rubbed the back of his neck where the Roman had hit him. It hurt horribly.

The Roman blew between closed lips, so that they made a blubbery whisper. Then he took his pistol in his right hand and stood up.

Roberto tensed for action. He had nothing, nothing he could use to defend himself. But he could run for the bushes if he had to.

The Roman pulled a bit of ripped cloth from inside his duffel bag. He walked backward to the water, stooped, and twisted just enough to dip the cloth in the river. Then he squeezed the dripping cloth and handed it to Roberto. "Put it here." He pointed at Roberto, then at the back of his own neck, then back to Roberto. "Go on." He gestured over and over. "Go on."

Roberto took the cloth. It was freezing cold. He held it to the back of his neck and kept his eyes on the gun.

The Roman squatted. He ran his hand wearily from his forehead down his cheek and across his mouth. "Poor dumb Slavs. Look what Stalin did. All the farmers are off in Siberia and the people left behind have nothing to eat." He took a box of biscuits out of his duffel bag. He opened it and tossed one to Roberto. He took a bite of his, then locked eyes with Roberto for the first time. "I can't believe you fight so well on empty stomachs." He brushed biscuit crumbs from his jacket front and sat on the ground again.

Roberto's fingers closed tight around the biscuit. He

didn't know anything about Stalin, really. He'd heard the name in school, of course—Stalin was the Soviet dictator. But he didn't know Stalin had sent farmers from around here to Siberia. He didn't know that was the cause of the famine. He thought about the abandoned buildings in the town last night and again in the settlement he'd seen on the river today. Those empty homes were evidence of misery—like so many graves. The people in this part of Ukraine were starving.

And, oh, how had his boy managed to get hold of that big sweet bun? In a burst of clarity Roberto realized that he must have used his ingenuity to get the bun—maybe he'd even stolen it—just to make Roberto's guard so hungry he left his post. That's why the boy hadn't taken a bite, but only sniffed the bun loudly. He probably had to sneak the bun back to where he'd stolen it before it was missed. The boy had risked a lot in order to help Roberto escape.

How strange life was. The boy was Roberto's friend. A Ukrainian friend.

Roberto hoped with all his heart that his boy and all the people he'd seen today wouldn't starve.

What was wrong with Stalin to have starved his own people?

What was wrong with the world?

Roberto's neck hurt less now, but his head hurt instead. He didn't want to think anymore. He gnawed on the hard biscuit. It was slightly sweet. It soothed him. He felt himself falling asleep.

The Roman kicked Roberto's shoe.

Roberto blinked and pulled his knees to his chest.

"May God forgive me. But I have no choice. Kid or no kid, that's how it is."

The words horrified Roberto. What was the Roman going to do to him? He squeezed his arms tight around his knees.

The Roman stood up and tied his duffel closed. Then he pointed at Roberto. "I saw you paddle." He gestured paddling the boat. "Get your boat. We can be in Romania in a day and a half, the way you paddle." He pointed his pistol at Roberto with his right hand, and with his left he pointed at the bush where the boat was hidden. "Put that boat in the water." His voice was rough now. He gestured paddling again.

Roberto stood slowly, keeping his eyes on the pistol. He pulled out the boat. He was exhausted, and now that he was standing, he felt slightly faint. He didn't believe he could paddle for more than ten minutes without falling asleep.

"Hurry."

Roberto couldn't hurry. He could barely move.

It was so late.

And it was so hot. Just like that, the world had turned hot.

Roberto took off his hat and threw it in the bottom of the boat. The wind off the water felt good on his bare head. It helped to cool him. He wondered suddenly if he should have acted as though he didn't understand what the Roman wanted. He glanced sideways at him. But the Roman was looking out across the water, scanning for movement.

"Hurry." The Roman helped slide the boat into the water. He looked all around one last time; then he got in and lay on his back with his knees bent. From outside the boat no one could see him. He held the pistol with both hands, aimed at Roberto's chest.

Roberto knelt in the stern and leaned over the side. He splashed his face with seawater. The shock of the freezing water helped to wake him. He paddled hard. The pain in his neck burned again. In fact, his whole chest burned. It must be the air. How could the air off the Black Sea be so warm when the water was freezing? Just this morning everything had been cold.

"Don't think of pulling any fast ones. I can see the tops of the trees on this shore." The Roman pointed to his eyes, then to the trees, then back to himself and then back to the trees again. "If you try to cross the river to Nikolajev, I'll know." He slapped his pistol as if it alone could make Roberto understand what he said. "Don't make me shoot you." His voice broke. "Oh, Christ, please don't make me shoot a kid."

Roberto paddled. They made it out of the harbor and turned west to stay along the north shore of the Black Sea. There was no sign of life anywhere. That was a blessing because Roberto could hardly see in the rapidly deepening night. He could hear his blood pounding in his ears. And he was hot and getting hotter every moment. He put down his paddle and pulled off his outer sweater.

"Paddle!"

Roberto paddled. He licked his lips. They were so cracked now, the skin curled out in thin chips. He blinked and paddled. Where were the other soldiers from this Roman's troop? Would they shoot on sight? He wanted to hide in the bottom of the boat, like the Roman.

Hours passed. Roberto didn't know where his energy came from. It was as though he paddled in his sleep. But at least he was paddling in the right direction. If he ever managed to get away from this soldier, he'd be closer to Italy.

It was black night now. He looked up. There were no stars behind them. The eastern sky was as cloudy as before a storm. But it should have been colder if a storm was coming. Instead, it was so hot. Roberto's back ached. His neck ached. His arms were beyond feeling. He paddled and paddled.

"Good. We're going good." The Roman's voice trembled a little. "This is crazy, taking a kid away from his home—

his country. What am I thinking?" He cleared his throat. Roberto could see the outline of the pistol in the dim moonlight. "I only need you till Romania." The Roman spoke in a strained, quiet voice. Roberto could hardly hear him. "From there I can go it alone. You can turn the boat around then and go back. That's it. You'll make it home again, I'm sure. You'll make it." He rested the gun on his belly.

A light appeared up ahead. And another. Scattered twinkles lined the shore. Roberto wiped his brow. He was sweating. He looked down at the Roman again.

The Roman stared at him, the whites of his eyes glistening through the dark. From where he lay he couldn't see the cultivated fields, which were already beside them, the buildings ahead. He had no idea they were approaching a town.

Roberto thought of pointing to warn the Roman. After all, the Roman had fed him. But, then, the Roman needed him to paddle the boat—that's probably why he fed him. Would Roberto be better off if the Roman knew about the town or not? He was too tired to try to figure it out. So he just paddled. Paddled and paddled.

Sweat dripped down his temples. He could feel that his shirt, inside the one sweater he still wore, was soaked through, but he didn't dare stop to take off the other sweater. He paddled. And now they were passing the first houses, dark and silent in the night. Roberto wiped the sweat out of his eyes. He thought he heard the brief lowing of cattle, but it might have been only the wind on the water, the wind, which was behind them, helping to move the boat. They skimmed along, the houses thick together now and a wall of sandbags in front of them all.

Sandbags. A wall against bullets. Everywhere Roberto went he was surrounded by war. He leaned over the side and splashed his face again. He watched the shore carefully. If he was going to have any chance at escape, he had to stay alert.

He paddled. His wet hands were slippery on the handle of the paddle. He was bathed in sweat. But he kept his eyes on the shore.

A bright light flashed on him from ahead and above. The danger came from the water, not the shore! How could he have not heard it approach? Roberto stared into the light of the patrol boat with a feeling of doom. Someone shouted at him in Ukrainian.

"Don't let them know I'm here!" said the Roman. "Don't let them kill me."

Roberto couldn't see the Roman's face because of the glare of the boat light. He couldn't see his gun, but he knew it was still pointed at him. He had to think hard. And fast. He didn't want anyone to die.

The light moved down the boat. As it left Roberto, he

swung the paddle and knocked the pistol from the Roman's hand. Roberto reached down and grabbed the pistol. The Roman was in full light now, curled on his side in the bottom of the boat, as though hunching that way would make him invisible. There were more shouts in Ukrainian.

Roberto stood in the boat with the balance of a *gondoliere*'s son. He leaned over the Roman and pointed the pistol at him, in full view of the patrol boat. The Roman stared at Roberto with desperation in his eyes. Roberto turned his face into the light and smiled. He waved his pistol at the men in the patrol boat. He was blinded by the light, but he smiled as wide as he could. He felt oddly euphoric. Invulnerable. He laughed.

Then he stuck the pistol in his waistband. He pulled his peasant hat out from under the Roman's leg and slapped it on his head. He picked up his paddle. It almost slipped from his hands, they were so wet with sweat. But he caught it just in time. He waved the paddle at the patrol boat and smiled crazily and paddled.

The men in the patrol boat spoke quickly, several voices interrupting one another.

Roberto paddled past them. He waved again. He paddled. Their light followed him. He didn't look back. His head spun. After a few minutes, the light turned away.

Could it have worked? Or would he be shot from behind?

Roberto paddled. He couldn't see the Roman lying in the bottom of the boat. He couldn't hear the splash of the water. He couldn't feel the wood in his hands. It was as though his senses had died. He paddled and paddled and paddled, until he fell forward onto the Roman in a black, black world.

STONES

"Easy, take it easy." The Roman held
Roberto's head in his lap and put a canteen to his lips.
"That's a bad wound. Very bad, kid."

Roberto drank. The metallic-tasting water dribbled
down his chin. He shivered. Dawn lightened the sky.
Roberto breathed through his mouth and blinked at the rising sun. Now he realized he wore only his shirt. The left
sleeve had been ripped open and the bandage had been re-
moved. The dark, swollen bullet wound oozed. He grazed
it with his fingertips. Even that slight touch sent knives of
pain up his arm, through his armpit, across his chest. He
tried to sit up. His stomach heaved. He sank back.

The Roman soldier held the canteen for him again.
Then he capped it and eased himself out from under
Roberto's head. He spread out Roberto's two sweaters and

rolled them into a tube shape. He lifted Roberto's head tenderly and slipped the sweaters under as a pillow. "There. That should make it a little better." He stretched and yawned. "I feel as stiff as after I've been up all night driving." He went to the stern of the boat, knelt, and paddled. He was a lousy paddler. No wonder he had taken Roberto along to paddle. No wonder.

Roberto faded out.

When Roberto came to again, he could tell by the sky that it was midmorning. He sat up. A moan escaped him.

Roberto looked around. The boat was tied by a rope to a stick that served as a stake, shoved into the ground on the bank. And the boat wasn't on the sea anymore; it rocked in the slow waters of a small creek. He shivered. He was naked to the waist.

The Roman lay on the ground beside the stake and rubbed the sleep from his eyes. He yawned and smiled. "Everything looks better after a little sleep, no?" He pulled the stake out, and threw it in the boat. Then he got in and felt Roberto's forehead. "I shouldn't be doing this. I should have just left you on the shore." He gave a long whistle and smiled again. "I think I'm going crazy." His tone was cheerful, despite his words. He carefully helped Roberto into one of the sweaters. The action hurt horribly, as though his arm would split from the pressure. Roberto cried out. The Roman winced. "If the fever doesn't come back, we'll give you the other sweater."

He opened his duffel bag and took out a square can and a can opener. He searched around and came up with a fork. He fed a forkful of beans to Roberto, then to himself. He alternated back and forth till the can was empty. He filled his canteen in the creek and helped Roberto drink. The water was slightly brackish, but not terrible. Roberto drank as much as he could hold. Then the Roman finished the canteen. He filled it again, closed it, and put it in the duffel. He pulled out the box of biscuits and handed one to Roberto. The Roman whistled. "A full belly helps the world look better, too."

Roberto gnawed on the biscuit. He lay back in exhaustion.

The Roman sat on the bottom of the boat with his right elbow on one knee and his face resting in his right hand. His face went serious. "That was some stunt back at Odessa. You surprised me. I don't know why you did it, but you've sure got guts." He looked off. "What now? What do we do with you, kid? I can talk myself blue in the face, but I don't find any answers. I have no idea."

Roberto panted. The heat returned to his face. He felt beads of sweat on his forehead.

The Roman didn't seem to notice. He looked up and down the creek and the shoreline. He took the paddle and went to the stern of the boat. He paddled furiously.

Roberto could tell from the change in the movement of the water that the boat had entered the sea again. He could tell from the sun that they were continuing west. At least that much was in his favor. He tried to sit up. His arm hurt so badly he screamed.

The Roman let out a little cry of sympathy. He put down the paddle and felt Roberto's hot face. He shook his head. Then he pulled off Roberto's sweater, going gingerly over the wound. He picked up a wad of material that Roberto now realized was his own shirt and dipped it in the water. He swabbed Roberto's head and chest and arms. And all the time he worked, he chewed on his bottom lip. "Once we get to Romania, we'll get you to a hospital for prisoners of war. Yes, that's the only answer. Yes."

The Roman went back to the stern and paddled fast.

Roberto wanted to shake his head, but his neck hurt too much to move it. He didn't want to be a prisoner of war. He moaned.

"Damn." The Roman paddled faster.

Roberto moaned as his head lolled about.

The Roman suddenly stopped and looked at him with the saddest face in the world. "I don't know anything about medicine." He opened his canteen and forced water down Roberto's throat. He took a knife out of his pocket. "But I know more about war than I ever wanted to know. If I turn

you over, if you're lucky, they'll chop off your arm and you'll
have a fifty-fifty chance of dying slowly of infection from
the amputation."

The terrifying image squeezed Roberto's heart hard,
then floated away, as if it were a memory. The pain in his
arm wiped out all thought.

"If you aren't lucky, they'll shoot you." The Roman took
a box of matches from his duffel. "And I haven't seen too
many lucky prisoners of war so far." He lit a match and ran
the flame along the blade of the knife. "God help me." He
gritted his teeth, grabbed Roberto's arm by the wrist, and
made a quick slash through the bullet wound.

Roberto threw himself away from the immense pain. He
could hardly breathe. His tears flowed. His nose ran.

But already the pain was changing. Roberto no longer
felt like he was about to explode. Instead, he just ached.
He ached and ached. The Roman pressed on the wound
from both sides and pus and blood rolled down Roberto's
arm. When the pink turned to dark red, the Roman doused
Roberto's arm with seawater. He doused it over and over
again. When he finally let go, Roberto turned his head away
and slept.

Roberto opened his eyes to the flat, early afternoon sky.
The Roman was looking at him while paddling steadily.
Without a word, he lay the paddle down and dipped the

shirt over the side of the boat. He doused Roberto's arm. Then he felt his forehead. A grin broke out across his face. "You're actually cool now. Cold even." He laughed in happy relief. "Oh, thank God. If we don't put some clothes on you soon, you'll take a chill."

Roberto propped himself up on his right elbow. His chest was all gooseflesh. He looked at his arm. The Roman had ripped part of Roberto's shirt into strips and tied three of them around the arm at equal intervals to hold the sides of the incision together. The cut was dark and caked with blood. But it wasn't bleeding anymore. And there was no sign of swelling.

"We'll wrap a blanket around you and keep your arm sticking out. It'll dry that way. Then if it doesn't swell, that'll be it." The Roman didn't look at Roberto as he talked. He was happy enough having a conversation with himself. "Dr. Maurizio to the rescue. If only Mamma could see me now. She always said I should have been a doctor." He laughed again. "Me, a doctor." He pulled a wool blanket out of his duffel and tucked it around Roberto's chest, under his chin, and around his back. He whistled as he worked.

Roberto lay back, grateful for the warmth of the blanket.

The Roman helped Roberto drink from the canteen. "While you were sleeping, we passed the harbor at Costanta. We made good time because of the sandbars. The whole shoreline is dotted with sandbars that keep out the waves." The Roman smiled. "And the wind was behind us. That helped, too." He smoothed Roberto's blanket and seemed to be a new person—lighthearted and loquacious— a chatterbox, even. "What a joke Costanta's port is—it's practically nothing compared to Rome's. Anyway, another patrol boat stopped us. I played our trick—I was the soldier and you were my prisoner. We were lucky to be in Romania—an Axis country. They respect an Italian uniform. They might be the only people left in Europe who do." He gave a bitter laugh. "One of their military boats escorted us past the harbor. They gave me two potato cakes." He reached into his duffle. "Here's yours." He fed Roberto the potato cake.

"Thank you," said Roberto, swallowing the last of the cake. His voice came out hoarse.

The Roman stared. "You're Italian."

"Venetian."

The Roman sank back on his heels, stunned. "Who are you?"

"Roberto. And I take it you're Dr. Maurizio."

Maurizio laughed. "So you've got a sense of humor." All at once he blushed. "We could have been talking, instead of you listening to me babbling to myself like a madman."

"You didn't sound like a madman."

"It's okay. I've done it all my life—whenever I'm scared, I just talk." Maurizio gave a quick nod. "But tell me: Who are you? How did you get here?"

And so Roberto told him. Everything.

Maurizio paddled as Roberto talked, scanning the shore and the sea regularly. He interrupted him only twice—once to check the wound and once to help him into his sweaters and tuck the blanket back into the duffel. When Roberto finished, Maurizio said, "While you've been talking, we've traveled the whole shoreline of Bulgaria. It's short, that's true. But I'm still amazed. Either we're ridiculously lucky or they're bunglers at war. How's your arm?"

Roberto smiled. "Better." He looked up at billowing black clouds. He remembered the east sky the night before—how it had been starless. "The rain's finally catching up with us."

Maurizio jerked to attention. "What?"

"See?" Roberto pointed. "It's slow, but that rainstorm has been following us since last night. You could tell from the sky."

"Maybe you could tell," said Maurizio, with an edge in his voice. "I couldn't. We've got to get to shore." He turned the boat to cut across the waves and paddled fiercely.

The clouds raced now, as though the storm had a burst of new energy. Roberto pushed himself up on his elbows. He could see the wall of gray rain press toward them.

And suddenly the rain was upon them in fat, heavy, pounding drops. Lightning cracked close by. Maurizio paddled harder than ever. He threw his whole body into every stroke.

The boat bottom caught on the sand. Maurizio jumped out and leaned over Roberto. "Can you get out by yourself?" he shouted over the wind.

"I think so."

"Hurry then."

Maurizio grabbed the duffel and balanced it on his head. He carried it onto the shore. Roberto climbed out and stood in shin-high water, fighting the waves to hold on to the boat. Hateful pain ripped through his arm, but he wouldn't let go. The rain pelted his face and soaked him to the bone. Maurizio ran back and pulled the boat up out of the water. Together they turned it upside down and shoved it under bushes at the edge of what looked like a fairly dense forest. Then they pushed the duffel and the paddle under and crawled in themselves.

Roberto rolled onto his back, exhausted. He felt the hot blood run from his wound. He must have knocked it open in all the rushed activity. It was dark as night under the boat. He was cold, bitterly cold. The wind howled. The rain banged on the underside of the boat.

Maurizio groaned. "Everything hurts. My hands, my back. I can't begin to think what you must feel like."

"I'm okay," lied Roberto.

Maurizio gave a small laugh. "And I can swim like a fish."

"You can't swim?"

"Not a stroke." Maurizio laughed more. Then he fell silent.

Roberto huddled up against him for warmth. "If we're ever in a storm again and the boat turns over, grab on to the side. The boat won't sink. I swear."

"Okay. I'll remember that."

"And . . ."

"Hush!" Maurizio clapped his hand over Roberto's mouth and pressed hard.

And now Roberto heard them, too. Voices. German words. Roberto slowly turned his head away from Maurizio's hand so that he could peer out under the tilted-up edge of the boat. But he couldn't see a thing—everything was dark and lost in the rain. The voices rose in heated discussion, clear and loud. They couldn't have been more than a few meters in front of the boat. So many voices— a troop of maybe two dozen. Had they seen Roberto and Maurizio come to shore? Were they looking for them? Still more voices came, and now from behind the boat. There were Germans everywhere. They were surrounded.

Roberto trembled, now more from fear than cold. Even if the Germans weren't looking for them, someone was bound to stumble over the boat in this blinding rain. Roberto drew his knees up and twisted onto his right side and stared out at the bouncing drops. The Germans kept talking—talking and talking. Roberto gathered his energy and waited.

Maurizio curled around him from behind and put his arm across him. Roberto could smell the sourness of fear in his breath. He could feel the tension in his arm. They lay together like hunted animals in a lair.

Finally the voices seemed to move away. Yes, the Germans were leaving. And now Roberto couldn't hear them anymore. Had they really left? It was getting late and the rain wasn't letting up—maybe the German troops had decided to camp for the night in these woods. That would be a sensible thing to do. Maybe they had moved away only a few meters. If they camped close by, they would find Roberto in the morning. They would find him. His jaw hurt from tension. His shoulders ached. He was tight and hard everywhere. He stared into the rain.

They would find him.

The rain fell. The ground turned to mud under Roberto's cheek. Everything slowly went soft. Night came.

When Roberto woke, he knew instantly that Maurizio was gone. He recognized that sensation of being utterly alone, even before he remembered where he was. He ran his hands frantically along the hardening mud. His fingers closed around the thin neck of the paddle. At least he had the paddle.

He listened closely. Nothing but the sound of birds. He peeked out from under the edge of the boat. The sun dazzled him. He blinked and edged himself along until his whole head stuck out.

The blanket was stretched over a bush, drying. The other contents of the duffel sat here and there in the sun.

"They left at dawn." Maurizio appeared from around the end of the boat. "Take your sweaters off to dry. The rest of your clothes can dry on your back."

Roberto came out, stood, and stretched. "They were near."

"Very near. I think you're my lucky charm, Roberto." Maurizio smiled. Then his face went solemn. "But luck can't hold forever."

Roberto took off his sweaters and draped them over bushes. Then he and Maurizio sat on the ground side by side.

"It's time to figure things out," said Maurizio. "We're only a few hours from the strait."

The strait—the gateway to the Mediterranean, at last. "Didn't Turkey stay neutral in the war?"

"Last I heard."

"Well, then," said Roberto in confusion, "what do we have to figure out?"

"What we're going to do—each of us."

Roberto's heart lurched. "Each of us? We should stay together, whatever we do."

Maurizio didn't answer.

"Dressed the way we are, we can pass through any waters—taking turns acting as the captor and captive." Roberto's words tumbled out. Then suddenly it hit him: Maurizio's actions didn't make sense. The pain in Roberto's arm must have clouded his thinking from the very minute he met Maurizio—nothing Maurizio had done made sense; he could see that now. Maurizio was an Italian soldier, and Bulgaria had signed the Tripartite Pact. Bulgaria was with the Axis forces. Maurizio didn't have to hide from the Bulgarians when they passed the Bulgarian shore the day before. And Maurizio didn't have to hide from the German soldiers the night before. "Why didn't you go into a Bulgarian port? Why didn't you join those German soldiers?" Roberto moved on his butt away from Maurizio until he was facing him. "Did you do it for me? Because they'd arrest me for deserting?" His heart sped. His words tumbled out faster and faster. "How much food do you have left? Could we camp here, just till my arm heals, and then we can part ways? Please."

"Shhhh." Maurizio patted Roberto's shoulder. "They'd never arrest you. You're a kid. They'd arrest me."

"You? Why?"

"I'm the deserter."

The deserter. Now it fit together. All at once, all of it fit together.

Maurizio leaned forward, his elbows on his knees. "I joined up willingly." He spoke vaguely, like an old man. "My country was at war, and Mussolini was inspiring. I trained like a fiend. I was the perfect fascist. I don't know what was on my mind. It's not like I was blind and deaf. I saw them round up the Jews in Rome and put them in a ghetto. I heard how whole families shared a room and there were almost no bathroom facilities. But I just didn't think about it. I was so stupid. Can you believe I was that stupid? Can you believe me?"

Roberto blinked the burn from his eyes. The ghetto in Venice was old—Jews had lived there for centuries. They loved living there—it was beautiful and quiet. He realized now that he hadn't had any idea of what it meant when he'd read about Jews being gathered into ghettos in other parts of Italy. It was easy to be stupid. "Yes. I believe you."

"I got on that train up through Germany and across Poland with pride in my heart. And that's when I saw them. At first I was shocked at the women and children, running up to the train every time we stopped, begging. Standing there in dirty rags."

Roberto nodded. He reached into his pocket. The Polish girl's gift stone was still there.

"After a while I didn't see their faces anymore—they were just floods of people. We passed Jews pushed along and beaten. Most of them with hardly a rag on their backs. This was what I went to war for?" Maurizio pounded his fists on the ground. "No, this was nothing like it was supposed to be. I saw a troop of Hungarian boys being whipped about their legs. The blood ran down in stripes."

Roberto swallowed. He knew what those Hungarian boys were thinking, what they were feeling. Hungary was aligned with Germany, just like Italy. But alignments meant nothing in this war.

"By the time we reached Russia, I was unsure of everything. And then we took Rostov. There were so many bodies. The Germans fought the Soviets, but the Italians, we were stupefied at the masses of bodies. It didn't matter who was German and who was Soviet. Everything was strange and crazy. No one could think about who to kill; there were too many corpses to bury." Maurizio reached out and took Roberto's hand. "And so many of them were kids. They hadn't even started shaving yet."

Roberto squeezed Maurizio's hand.

A sob escaped Maurizio. "We moved on to Stalingrad,

burning every school we passed, every barn, burning almost anything of value—numb now—unthinking. The huge city fought fiercely. We cut them off from all supplies. It was so damn cold already. We made forts in the snow out of fallen trees. Even the tanks froze up. We had the city without food, without water. And you know what the German lieutenant said? He said we should let the whole city starve. He said that's what Hitler had ordered." Maurizio stopped talking. His shoulders shook with silent sobs.

Roberto hung his head. He folded his hands, fingers intertwined, as though he were praying. His hot tears fell on his own hands.

"We deserted. Lots of us. Most followed the Don River back toward Rostov, but I set out across the land for Nikolajev. And that's when I found you." Maurizio sat up tall. "If they catch me, I'll be shot."

"What will happen to you when you get back to Italy?"

"If I get back." Maurizio stood up. He brushed off his hands. Then he turned the boat over. "You hungry yet?" He grinned at Roberto. "That was a joke. I know you're starving."

Roberto reached for a can of food. He tossed it from hand to hand. "You're not going back to Italy, are you?"

"Yes, I am."

"You'll get shot."

"I'm not going to turn myself in. I'm joining the *partigiani*."

Roberto caught the can in one hand and handed it to Maurizio. "Who are they?"

"People against this war."

"My mother marched in a protest against the war. I guess she's a *partigiana*."

"Maybe. But if she was truly active, you'd have known it. The *partigiani* sabotage the war."

Roberto's scalp tingled. He hated this war. He hated all war. "How?"

Maurizio opened the can. He searched around through the stuff and came up with the fork. "Here. You go first." He handed the open can and fork to Roberto.

"Tell me. How do the *partigiani* sabotage the war?"

"With counter-guerilla activities—little mini-wars."

Roberto shook his head. He would never shoot at anyone in his life. He knew this now, without a shred of doubt. "So they're murderers, too."

"No." Maurizio's voice rose. Then he sighed. "I guess it depends on how you look at it. But you don't have to carry a rifle to be a *partigiano*. There are lots of them—and they don't all agree with each other. They do all kinds of things."

"Tell me."

"They blow up bridges. They demolish ammunitions factories. They derail trains."

Roberto thought of the burned reaper and tractor in the field outside his boy's village. "Is everything they do destructive?"

"They smuggle Jews from one hiding place to another."

A prickle of fearful hope climbed Roberto's spine. "Yes."

"Yes what?"

"I'm going to be a *partigiano*."

"You're a kid."

"I know about war."

Maurizio rubbed at his bottom lip. "The *partigiani* run a lot of risks—and they suffer. They make trips over the Alps, dodging border controls, in the coldest weather."

Roberto thought of how he'd hidden himself under the snow as the soldiers passed by just days ago. "I can manage cold." He passed the half-eaten can of beans to Maurizio.

"Think of last night." Maurizio's eyes were hard. "The *partigiani* are the target of every German soldier."

"What about Italian soldiers?"

"Half the *partigiani*, maybe more, are deserters from the army. Most of the Italian soldiers look the other way. They pretend they don't see the bonfires."

"The bonfires?"

"That's how the *partigiani* send messages. They build bonfires on hills, and people know whether or not it's safe to gather or to go ahead with plans."

"I know how to build fires now."

"Yes, I know. You told me." Maurizio ate the rest of the beans in a couple of bites. He threw the can under a bush. "The *partigiani* are suspicious of outsiders. It'll be hard to convince them to let us help."

"We can do it."

"Yes, we can." Maurizio and Roberto shook hands. Then Maurizio looked around. "Help me find those biscuits. We need all the energy we can get. Our real work is just about to begin. Ah, here they are." He opened the box, took a biscuit for himself, and handed one to Roberto. "This work is going to be harder than anything else you or I have ever done."

Power surged through Roberto—the power of a strong spirit, as Samuele would have said. Power enough to share. "Feel this stone?" Roberto took the gift stone from the Polish girl out of his pocket. He held out his hand. "Feel it."

Maurizio touched the smooth stone.

"All you need is stones, Maurizio. If you have enough stones and the water is shallow enough, you can build a city up through the waves. Like Venice."

Maurizio looked at Roberto in confusion.

"I'm going to be a stone, Maurizio. I'll be part of the new city. You'll be a stone, too."

Maurizio nodded. "I guess I see what you mean."

Roberto smiled. "Want me to tell you stories as we paddle along? They help, I swear."

Maurizio laughed. "Why wait till we get in the boat? Start now."

"Once upon a time there was a hunchback boy." Roberto talked on as they sat in the sun, with their things drying around them. He rubbed the gift stone in his hands and spoke of sprouting wings.